DEEP AND DEADLY

The Black Dragon's divers chained a large block of metal to Tom's feet.

"That's to make certain that you sink quickly enough," Tom heard the Black Dragon say over the earphone. "It's very important that you reach the proper depth before the explosion takes place."

"You're insane," Tom gasped.

"Maybe," the Black Dragon said. "But it really doesn't matter to you anymore."

Soon they came to an area of the ocean floor where black plumes of superheated water rose out of underground springs. Around the fissures flourished a huge colony of tube worms—ten-foot-long creatures whose bloodred bodies swayed, snakelike, in the ocean currents.

Again the Black Dragon's voice sounded in Tom's ear. "If you have any last words, you ought to say them now." He set the timer on the bomb.

"Goodbye, Tom."

Books in the Tom Swift® Series

#1 THE BLACK DRAGON
#2 THE NEGATIVE ZONE
#3 CYBORG KICKBOXER
#4 THE DNA DISASTER
#5 MONSTER MACHINE
#6 AQUATECH WARRIORS

Available from ARCHWAY Paperbacks

TOM SWIFT

6

AQUATECH WARRIORS

VICTOR APPLETON

AN ARCHWAY PAPERBACK
Published by POCKET BOOKS

New York   London   Toronto   Sydney   Tokyo   Singapore

AN ARCHWAY PAPERBACK *Original*

An Archway Paperback published by
POCKET BOOKS, a division of Simon & Schuster Inc.
1230 Avenue of the Americas, New York, NY 10020

Copyright © 1991 by Simon & Schuster Inc.

Produced by Byron Preiss Visual Publications, Inc.
Special thanks to James D. MacDonald and Debra Doyle

ISBN: 0-671-67828-0

First Archway Paperback printing December 1991

10 9 8 7 6 5 4 3 2 1

TOM SWIFT, AN ARCHWAY PAPERBACK and colophon
are registered trademarks of Simon & Schuster Inc.

Cover art by Carla Sormanti

Printed in the U.S.A.

IL 6+

YOU SAID WE WERE GOING ON A TROPICAL vacation," Rick Cantwell grumbled good-naturedly to his friend Tom Swift. "You never said you were taking us sailing into the middle of the Bermuda Triangle."

Tom laughed. "I said subtropical," he pointed out. "Bermuda's on about the same latitude as Charleston, South Carolina. If this were the real tropics, the temperature wouldn't be nearly this comfortable. Besides, right now we aren't sailing; we're sitting still forty miles east of Bermuda."

"The problem with you is that you're too literal-minded sometimes," said Rick. In spite of his words, a smile creased his broad face. "But for a stretch of water that's supposed to be haunted or infested with sea monsters or something, this place isn't half bad."

It was indeed a fine day at sea. The sun

1

shone warmly out of a cloudless sky above the Swift Enterprises oceangoing experimental platform. Small waves rolled out of the south. Far out where the ocean met the sky, a faint haze of humidity gave the horizon a bluish tinge. A light breeze, south by west, ruffled Tom's blond hair. Polarized sunglasses shaded his blue eyes from the glare reflected off the water.

From where he stood on the deck of the experimental platform, Tom could look in all directions without seeing a hint of land or of any other vessel. The platform itself, a rectangular, bargelike structure about one hundred feet wide by two hundred feet long, lay dead still in the ocean in spite of the waves breaking against its windward side.

Tom and his father had designed the floating platform to provide support for very deep sea exploration and scientific experiments. In addition to a scientific team, it carried a captain and a crew of four. Tom was on board the platform during its sea trials as the technical representative of Swift Enterprises, in charge of the final testing of all the machinery and systems.

Like an iceberg, most of the platform's volume lay beneath the surface of the water. Its computer-controlled stabilizing fins kept the vessel in place and motionless. Water jets on all sides counteracted the effects of wind and current. Far belowdecks, underneath the crew's living spaces and the scientific laboratories, pumps constantly shifted the liquid ballast to keep the platform from rolling with the waves.

Above the water, the forward part of the platform was largely empty space, painted with the cross-and-circle pattern of a helicopter landing pad. The after section of the platform sported a raised superstructure and an array of antennas. On a mast above the top level of the superstructure, above the bridge, a United States flag fluttered from the mast, with the Swift Enterprises flag flying just below it.

"You can forget about the Bermuda Triangle, anyway," Tom said to Rick. "It's all gossip and sensationalism."

"I guess you're right," said Rick. "Actually, this vacation's been pretty spiffy so far. Only one complaint—you said that there were going to be lots of good-looking girls where we were going, and so far I haven't seen any."

"I heard that!" called a feminine voice. "Aren't Sandra and I good enough for you?"

Mandy Coster stood about five feet away from Rick and Tom. A chest-high glass tank, four feet square and filled with seawater, was bolted to the deck between them. She wore a beach jacket over a blue tank top and shorts, with a dark blue bandanna tying back her chestnut hair, and she was smiling at Rick's embarrassed expression. Tom and Mandy had dated off and on, although there was no commitment on either part.

"Hey, don't get me wrong," Rick protested, red faced. "What I meant was, any *other* good-looking girls—"

"Quit while you're ahead," advised Sandra Swift as she came out the doorway of the platform's superstructure and joined the others on the deck.

Tom's younger sister was wearing a bright pink one-piece bathing suit and leather sandals. In one hand she carried a dull metal plate, about eight inches square by one-quarter-inch thick. With her free hand, she brushed a strand of sun-bleached hair back away from her eyes and added, "Or quit before you get too far behind, anyway."

Tom ignored their banter. "Sandra," he said, "did you bring the test plate?"

"I sure did," she replied, holding up the metal plate. "What do you think this is, a pizza?"

"I wish it were," said Rick. "Sea air makes me hungry all the time."

As Rick spoke, a lean, silver-haired man emerged from belowdecks. "Good day, my friends," he called out in a strong French accent. "How is it going this fine morning?"

"It's going great, Louis," said Tom. He pronounced the name in the French way, *Loo-ee*. "How are you?"

"Very fine, thank you." Louis Armont was

in his late sixties but still trim and muscular. He wore a pair of lime green swim trunks and a T-shirt that read "Oceanographers for a Better Planet." When he smiled, his tanned face broke into a multitude of lines and creases.

Armont looked from the metal plate to a small device in Tom's right hand. The device had a crystal face and was studded with an array of metal knobs and buttons.

"Ah," Louis said, "I see you are still at your experiments. If I did not know you better, I would say that you have there an ordinary diver's wristwatch."

"As a matter of fact," Tom said, "telling time is only one of the many things it does. I call it a chronolaser, and it's designed as a diver's all-purpose tool. It's a depth gauge, a signaling device, a remote controller, and a cutting implement."

"Indeed," Armont said. "It seems to me, young Tom, that you have a deadly weapon strapped onto your wrist."

"Think of it as a high-tech diver's knife," said Tom. "The laser's low-power setting isn't much stronger than the light from a flashlight, so you can aim the laser safely when you turn it on—and so nobody will get hurt if you turn it on by accident. We're going to check out the cutting function right now."

The young inventor strapped the watch to his left wrist. He turned back to Rick. "Ready?"

he asked. "Take that plate from Sandra and put it in the water there. Hold it by the edges, okay?"

"Sure, Tom," Rick said. He took the metal plate and carefully lowered it into the tank with both hands.

Tom put his left arm in the tank until the warm water came up to his elbow. A streak of light shone out of the chronolaser on Tom's wrist. Like a thin, glowing wire, the laser beam stretched across the tank to the metal plate Rick held in his hands.

Tom aimed the beam of light at the center of the steel plate Rick was holding. "Time to increase the settings."

The digital display on the chronolaser flickered to 2, then 3, then 4. The beam of light grew more intense, and where it touched the steel, the metal glowed a bright orange. After a few moments, the water next to that point on the plate started to boil, and clouds of bubbles streamed upward. When they burst, wisps of steam swirled above the surface of the tank.

"*C'est merveilleux!*" exclaimed Armont. "How did you do that without touching the device itself? You cannot be controlling the laser with thought waves, but—"

"Not thought waves exactly," Tom said. "Do you see the band that keeps the chronolaser strapped to my wrist? It's full of sensors. It detects the change in capacitance in my wrist, from just my tensing and relaxing my fingers. Controlling the chronolaser is sort of like playing the piano—or like programming a computer in sign language—and it should work even if there's a diving suit between the chronolaser and my wrist. Now to shut it off."

There was a pause. The beam of coherent light continued to show a bright red.

Tom frowned. "It should have gone off by now. Let me try it again."

The glow of the laser beam did not change.

"What is wrong, Tom?" asked Louis.

"I think it's the regulator circuits," said Tom. "They aren't responding properly."

"I hope you can do something about them before you burn all the way through the plate," Rick said with a nervous laugh. "Laser beams may pass through glass and water without hurting anything, but my own personal body is a different story."

"Let me try taking it down step by step," Tom said.

He frowned in concentration. The number on the chronolaser's face changed to a 5, and the beam's intensity increased again.

"It shouldn't have done that," Tom muttered. "It should have gone down, not up."

"Well, it went up," Rick said. "Tom, old buddy, don't forget I'm standing downrange of that thing."

"All you have to do is step aside if you're

worried," said Tom. "The beam isn't going to chase after you."

"But if the beam is still on at full power," said Sandra, "I don't see how you can take your hand out of the tank to fix the regulators. You might drill a hole clear through the platform—and through anybody who accidentally got in the way of the beam."

"Give me a moment," said Tom. "I'm thinking. . . . Mandy, lend me your pocket mirror, okay?"

Mandy pulled a small makeup compact out of the pocket of her beach jacket and handed it to Tom. "Here you are."

Tom took the compact with his free hand. "Thanks," he said. "Now everyone watch out."

He opened the compact. Turning it so that the mirror faced to his left at a forty-five-degree angle, he lowered it into the tank. Moving carefully but quickly, he slid the mirror into the path of the laser beam. The laser was reflected away from the metal plate, through the glass side of the tank. It traced its way forward, over the bow of the floating platform and safely out over the ocean.

"Great," Tom said. "That shouldn't drill any accidental holes. Now, Mandy, could you reach into the tank and unstrap the chronolaser?"

Mandy reached down into the water.

"Be very careful," Tom warned. "Don't get in the way of the beam."

"Don't worry," Mandy replied. A moment later, she said, "I've got it."

The moment the band came loose from Tom's wrist, the beam of light vanished.

Rick stared. "How'd you do that?"

"Without a signal coming from the sensors, it had to go out," Tom answered.

"And not a minute too soon," Rick said. He pulled the steel plate from the tank. The metal had cooled in beadlike droplets around the smooth, round hole the laser beam had cut nearly all the way through the plate.

"The salt water must have increased the interface conductivity," Tom said. He turned the chronolaser facedown and began to adjust a tiny rheostat on the back. "I'll just lower the sensitivity a bit, and it'll work fine under the sea." He finished making his adjustments and strapped the chronolaser back onto his wrist.

"When I was younger," said Louis, "I used to explore sunken ships, looking for treasure. Many times, then, did I wish for something like this." He laughed. "Now I am an oceanographer, not an adventurer. I leave the treasure for young people like you and hunt for knowledge instead."

"So how *is* your research going, Louis?" Tom asked.

"Very well. Very well indeed," the Frenchman replied. "This stable oceangoing platform of your father's is exactly what I needed."

Louis Armont and the two scientists in his research team were doing very detailed mapping of the bottom of the sea around Bermuda, using echolocation and computer-enhanced sonar imaging that would be blurred by any motion of the vessel on which the instruments were mounted. Tom Swift, Sr., had offered Armont the oceangoing platform as a base for his delicate measurements, both as a favor to a distinguished elder scientist and as a final test of the platform's stability.

"I think I have found something very unusual about the seabed here," Louis continued. "As you know, there is no other land for hundreds of miles in any direction. The seabed from which the Bermuda Rise comes is deep—thousands of feet deep—and then suddenly comes shoal water and the northernmost coral reef in the world."

" 'Full fathom five thy father lies,' " cut in a voice from above. " 'Of his bones are coral made.' "

Tom looked up to see the smiling, bearded face of Denny O'Brien, captain of the floating platform. O'Brien was standing on the bridge wing—the open catwalk that ran around the upper level of the superstructure.

" 'Those are pearls that were his eyes,' " O'Brien continued. "When Shakespeare wrote *The Tempest*, the magic island that he set it on was Bermuda. And there's mystery here, right enough. The Bermuda Triangle—"

Tom laughed. "Oh, come on. Don't tell me *you* believe in the Bermuda Triangle."

"No," said O'Brien, "but I do believe in high winds, heavy seas, shoal water, and sharks, all of which we have plenty of in these parts. And this year has been a bad one for missing ships. The latest Local Notice to Mariners just came in, and it requests that all vessels in the area be on the lookout for the *Chevalier* out of Glasgow. Overdue and presumed lost. That makes three ships missing in this month alone."

As if the captain's words had given the signal, an alarm bell began clamoring below-decks.

The platform rolled sharply on its starboard side. Water slapped over the rail to the windward. Then the deck plunged down in the opposite direction with a splash that sent white water geysering into the air.

"Hit the life raft!" O'Brien shouted from the bridge wing. "The stabilizer's gone!"

2

"MY DATA!" LOUIS ARMONT CRIED. HE RAN FOR the open door of the superstructure and vanished belowdecks.

The platform rolled the other way, thirty degrees or more. Tom found himself staring down at the dark blue surface of the ocean. He grabbed the rim of the saltwater tank with one hand to keep from losing his balance.

Water sloshed out of the tank, soaking Mandy's tank top and shorts. Spray flew.

"This way!" Tom shouted, pointing aft with his free hand. "We have to get to the emergency raft."

"I want to stay and help," Rick said.

"The captain said leave!" Tom said. "Come on!"

The platform started to roll heavily to port.

At the instant the deck was fairly level, Tom let go of the saltwater tank and dashed over to the side of the superstructure. The angle of the roll increased. He grabbed one of the metal handholds welded to the bulkhead. A second later he was joined by Rick, Mandy, and Sandra.

"Next time we're fairly level," said Tom, "make a run for the life raft."

"Hold tight!" Mandy cried. "Here we go again!"

The bow of the platform had buried itself in the sea. Now, as if lifted out, a solid wall of green water raced aft along the deck. The wall of water was about three feet high when it hit the place where the four teenagers were standing. It knocked Tom's feet out from under him and slammed him hard against the bulkhead.

Tom gripped the handhold even tighter as the water foamed past. The platform rolled again to starboard. At the limit of its roll, the platform hung motionless for a queasy, weightless instant that felt like forever to Tom. Then the deck was leveling out again, on its way into another heavy roll to port.

"Rick, go!" Tom called. "Start handing people down."

Rick sprinted to the raft, pulled the top hatch open, and jumped in. The platform's emergency raft looked like a thirty-foot-wide inner tube set into the deck of the platform. The raft's curved sides were shiny black like fresh paint, and its top was covered by an

International Orange panel to make it easy to spot from the air.

"Sandra, Mandy, you're next," Tom said. "Go!"

The two girls ran aft, struggling against the increasing slant of the deck, and scrambled into the raft. By then the slope was too great for Tom himself to make an attempt. The bulkhead he clung to was as close to level as the deck.

The port side of the platform crashed down into the water with a booming sound that Tom could feel vibrating up through the soles of his deck shoes. Three more people joined Tom at his handrail on the starboard side of the white-painted deckhouse: the two other members of Armont's scientific expedition— the tall, bearded father-and-son geophysicists, Matt and Bob Weinberg—plus Louis himself.

The Frenchman clutched a bright orange plastic case under one arm. "I have pulled all the data boards from my computers," he said. "Now I can leave."

Tom looked to starboard along the deck. It tilted uphill before him, and the railing was outlined starkly against the bright blue sky. He couldn't see the ocean or the horizon at all.

"We have to get away from the platform," Tom said. "It won't do anyone any good if we go down with it."

Once again, the platform rolled ponderously back to the level. Tom watched the deck come down. At twenty degrees of roll, he nodded at the three scientists.

"Go!"

The members of the scientific team ran to the raft and jumped in through the top hatch.

Tom looked around. No one else was in sight. He let go of the handrail and sprinted for the raft. The angle of the deck was changing under his feet as he ran. He leapt into the raft and pulled the hatch shut behind him.

"Stand by to launch. Launch!" Tom called out.

Sandra hit the Emergency Launch button.

The raft fell away from the bottom of the platform. Tom felt a jarring sensation as it hit and plunged below the surface of the water, and then another as it bobbed to the surface once again. In a moment, however, the raft leveled off, and the heavy rolling ceased.

"We're clear," announced Sandra Swift.

"Great," said Tom. "Stand by to pick up the skipper and the crew. If they can't save the platform, they'll expect us to rescue them."

He hurried over to the raft's command console. The inside of the raft was like a gigantic high-tech doughnut. An eight-foot-high ceiling curved down to the deck on either side, and the "room" itself circled out of sight in both directions. Swivel chairs were mounted on the plastic floor in front of banks of computers, monitors, and controls.

Viewports punctuated the bulkhead at regular intervals. Outside the raft, an unbroken expanse of blue-green water stretched out in all directions. In spite of the relatively calm ocean, however, the platform was still rolling heavily, yawing and pitching as if it were bucking huge waves instead of riding on a calm sea.

"What's going on out there?" Mandy asked. "And where are Captain O'Brien and the crew?"

"They're probably still working on damage control," said Tom. "Our job now is to stand by to pick them up if necessary. If O'Brien tells them to abandon the platform, we'll need to be ready."

He settled into the webbed chair in front of the controls, set his hands on the helm, and threw the throttle lever forward to start the engines. The habitat surged forward. Tom brought it around to circle the floating platform at high speed.

The platform kept up its heavy rolling for a few minutes longer. Then the vessel's violent motion ended as suddenly as it had begun.

Tom hit a switch in front of him to activate the habitat's external speakers. "Are you all right, Captain O'Brien?" he asked over the microphone.

His amplified voice boomed out across the

water. A minute later O'Brien came out onto the bridge wing, carrying a hand-held radio. A receiver on the habitat crackled to life, and O'Brien's voice came over a speaker on the command console.

"Tom, we've stabilized the platform for the moment. Request you check the bottom, over."

Tom switched his console microphone over to Radio. "This is Tom Swift," he said. "Roger your last, out."

He turned to his friends. "So, what do you think of the Swift Enterprises emergency habitat?"

"I thought you said this thing was a life-boat," Rick Cantwell replied, "not a floating palace."

"This is more than just a life raft," Tom explained. "It's an entire emergency habitat. It works best as a hovercraft—the jets are located outside, in the hole of the doughnut—but it can also cruise like a motorboat or submerge like a submarine."

"Why all the different options?" asked Mandy. "I know you like multipurpose designs on principle, but why in a life raft—excuse me, an emergency habitat?"

"The different options increase the passengers' chance of survival," Tom explained. "Say a ship with a Swift emergency habitat on board went down in a heavy storm. On the surface, the survivors could get battered to pieces by the waves. But if they submerged, they could get below the wave action and have a smooth ride until the storm passed. Or say a ship went aground in shallow water. In hovercraft mode, the habitat could get on top of the water or even cruise over a beach."

"This is great!" Mandy exclaimed. "You could explore the whole ocean from top to bottom in something like this."

"Actually," said Tom, "we've got a minisub berthed under the floating platform for times when we need to make really deep descents. The emergency habitat's safe down to only about five hundred feet. After that, the pressure might break the viewports."

"Are we going to take it under now?" Mandy asked.

"That's the fastest way I know to check things out beneath the platform," said Tom. "We could send out divers, but the suits are still—"

"You mean these suits?" Rick asked.

Tom's friend had been poking through a large locker near the main hatch. Now he held up a bright yellow suit of heavy plastic. One of several in the locker, all in different colors, the suit was meant to be worn with one of the clear plastic helmets that rested side by side in a row on the bottom of the locker. "This looks more like a space suit than a wet suit."

"They're my new experimental deep-diving suits," Tom said. "I haven't had a chance to field-test them yet. So right now, we'll just ride the habitat down."

Once again Tom began flicking switches. A low hum filled the habitat, and the floor vibrated faintly.

"Those are the motors on the compression tanks," Tom explained. "It'll just take a minute or two, and then we'll be ready to go."

"Look!" Mandy cried out, and pointed to the viewports.

The ocean had already begun to cover the habitat. Then, in a sudden swirl of water, they were completely submerged. Thousands of tiny bubbles filled the water around them. Sunlight filtered down in dancing patterns of blue-green and gold as the waves rippled and chopped above. A school of silvery fish, five inches long, scattered.

"How deep are we going?" Rick asked, watching their progress on the depth gauge.

"How about eighty feet?" Tom said.

Louis Armont was frowning slightly. "What about decompression?" he asked.

"No problem," said Tom. "The habitat is fully pressurized. It keeps us at normal sea-level pressure, just as a submarine would. No matter now deep we go, as long as we stay inside we'll be fine."

Outside the viewports the water cleared a bit, turning a deeper blue. Tom switched off the compressor's motors, and the habitat came to a stop.

Everyone—even Armont and his two assistants—crowded around the viewports to look out. Through the windows they could see the side of the platform, covered with intakes and jets for the propulsion system, and the vanes and sensors of the stabilizers. From this vantage point, they could see that underneath the flat top of the platform was a deep V-shaped hull, more like the bottom of a speedboat than that of a barge.

The light was a deep blue here, nearly one hundred feet down, and in the shadow of the platform, the sea was dark. "Let's take a look at things," Tom said as he flicked the switch marked Lights.

Bob Weinberg pointed at the bottom of the platform, now illuminated by the powerful floodlights at the front of the habitat. "What's that?" the geophysicist asked.

"Looks like a sheet of plastic," Tom said.

He brought the habitat closer and saw that his guess was right. A huge sheet of plastic covered all the sensors and water intakes across one side of the platform's hull.

Louis Armont sighed. "Someone must have thrown it from the side of a ship," he said. "When I was young, the oceans were so clean. I thought they would stay that way forever. Now diving in the sea is sometimes like swimming in a garbage dump. Trash is everywhere, even here."

"Maybe it was flotsam from a wreck or

something," Tom said. "It looks like more stuff was down there than just the plastic."

"What do you mean?" the Frenchman asked.

"I'm not seeing something that I should be seeing," said Tom. He pointed out the viewport at a wire hanging from the centerline of the platform's hull, along the keel. "Look at that cable. It should have a monitor camera on the end of it. The camera housing is about three feet across, and it just isn't there. Something must have snagged it and pulled it off."

"Or maybe the housing broke loose when we were doing all that rolling around," Matt Weinberg suggested. "It wouldn't surprise me at all."

"Me, either," said Tom. "Let's take a look."

He guided the habitat toward the place where the cable drifted gently in the ocean current. They drew closer and closer. There was a long pause.

"We've got problems," Tom said finally.

"Why's that?" Rick asked.

"That cable didn't break—it was cut."

CUT?" BOB WEINBERG REPEATED. "ARE YOU sure?"

"Perhaps not cut," Louis Armont said. "It is possible that a shark carried away the camera housing, thinking it was good to eat. Sharks are always hungry. There was one I recall, off Cape Finisterre, that bit right through a steel cable."

"You could be right," Tom said. He thought for a moment. "That camera was feeding information directly into the video data bank, recording the performance of the platform's stabilizers. When we get back onto the platform, we can check out anything it might have recorded before it came loose."

Tom maneuvered the habitat out from under the platform and back to the surface. Once on top of the water, the habitat started to bob and roll again. He guided the habitat up beside the platform, and Sandra opened the top hatch. Then she and Mandy climbed out to tie the habitat alongside the platform with nylon mooring lines.

Tom shut down the systems. "All right," he called. "Everybody out."

One by one they climbed from the habitat, Tom last of all. He shut the top hatch and locked it behind him. When he stepped aboard the platform, the deck felt odd beneath his feet. After a moment, he realized the difference: The platform no longer kept absolutely steady in the ocean. Instead, like any ordinary vessel, it rolled lightly with the movement of the waves.

Tom went over to the superstructure and climbed the ladder up to the pilothouse. As he'd expected, O'Brien was waiting for him.

"Well, Tom," the master mariner said, "now that we have things on an even keel again—what did you find down there?"

"Nothing good," Tom said. "There's a sheet of plastic covering a pretty fair part of the bottom on the starboard side. That might be what caused the stabilizers to go."

"Sounds likely," O'Brien said. "If the jets were covered, nothing would happen when the sensors detected motion and tried to correct for it."

"Right," said Tom. "Then the sensors would try even harder to correct the problem and start the platform rolling the other way. Then the platform would try to correct *that*, and so on and so on, setting up a nasty little negative feedback loop. That would explain why the rolls kept getting bigger, too."

O'Brien nodded. "It matches up with the way we eventually fixed the problem. We shut down the automatic stabilization routine, and the rolling damped itself right out. It was a freak accident. Nobody in the Swift Marine Engineering Department disposes of garbage over the side like that, but some people do. Now that we know what happened, we can send out divers to clear the junk away."

"Maybe that plastic wasn't just random garbage," Tom said. "The cable for the monitor camera may have been cut. Louis says it could have been a shark, though."

"One way to find out for certain," O'Brien said. "Let's check out the monitor record. We'll need to look at it anyway before we send out the divers."

The lean, tanned seafarer led the way down the bridge ladder to the main deck, then farther down belowdecks. On the second deck, he headed forward along a narrow passageway to a compartment labeled Monitoring Station.

O'Brien opened the door and walked in, with Tom close at his heels. The bulkhead of the monitoring station was covered with dials, gauges, digital readouts, and monitor screens. Computers and electronic equipment filled most of the available space.

"How's it going, Katie?" Captain O'Brien asked the sailor on duty.

"Pretty good, Skipper," the young woman replied. Like all the members of O'Brien's crew, Katie Booth was a longtime employee of the Marine Engineering Department of Swift Enterprises and a fully qualified sailor in her own right. "We've maintained watertight integrity, and the damage-control routines show no more than light damage from shifting equipment."

O'Brien glanced toward a readout still showing a yellow caution light. "What was our maximum roll?"

"Fifty-four degrees off the vertical," Katie replied. "I thought we were going over for sure."

"You weren't the only one," said Captain O'Brien. "Tom, maybe you should redesign the automatic stabilizer routine so we can shut it down from the bridge. We had to run all over the place taking pumps and motors off-line by hand. Katie, you and Jonesy see if you can jury-rig some sort of emergency override by tonight, okay?"

"Sure thing," Katie replied. She pulled a small green-backed notebook from her shirt pocket and scribbled a note. "Anything else?"

"One more thing," said O'Brien. "Tom and

I would like to see the last half hour of tape from the underwater monitor camera."

"No problem." Katie switched on a monochrome monitor and pressed a button on her control panel. "Coming up on screen one."

The screen showed nothing but static. "Take it back farther," Tom said.

Katie pushed a button marked Fast Rewind. For a long while nothing showed on the monitor. Then, abruptly, there came a flash of movement, followed by a view of the bottom of the platform, with no sign of the sheet of plastic.

"The camera gives a one-eighty-degree picture," Katie explained. "But it only points up because all we're interested in is how the control vanes move, clocked against actual water movement."

"Maybe the camera should have been pointed in another direction," Tom said, frowning at the screen. "Nothing there. Take it forward again slowly, to the point where we lost the picture."

Katie advanced the tape again. Nothing showed up. Then once again there was that flash of abrupt motion, and the picture went to snow.

"Whatever happened to the camera," Katie said, "happened before we started taking those rolls. The intakes were still clear in that picture, and the platform was as steady as a cornfield in Kansas."

"Single-step the tape back," Tom said. "I want to see what that thing was just before we lost the picture."

Katie started the picture back.

"There!" Tom said. "What's that?"

"Hard to say," O'Brien said, looking at the frozen picture on the monitor screen. "It's out of focus, whatever it is. That means it was close to the camera, but beyond that, I wouldn't like to guess."

"Could it be a shark, do you think?" Tom asked.

O'Brien studied the picture. "Hmmm. I can't say. It's not impossible."

"I can give you a digitized copy of this picture, if you want," Katie volunteered. "Maybe you could get Louis's computers to enhance the image."

"That's a great idea," said Tom. With a smile, he accepted the disk containing the digitized photo from Katie. Then he and O'Brien started back to the main deck.

"First step is going to be to remove that plastic sheet," O'Brien said. "But that could be risky if there's a shark still cruising about."

"I can handle sharks," Tom replied. "I've been looking for a chance to test my new diving suits anyway."

"Fine with me," O'Brien said. "We didn't suffer any major damage, but the crew and I will have our hands full topside checking things out and repairing the minor stuff. Just don't dive alone."

"Don't worry about that," Tom said. "I was thinking of taking Rick with me."

A few minutes later, Tom located Rick standing amid the wreckage of the cabin the two teenagers shared. Paper, clothing, and small pieces of experimental equipment lay scattered everywhere.

"Hey, Rick," Tom said. "How would you like to get out of this mess and go diving?"

Rick grinned. "I'm with you, Tom old buddy."

The two friends went out onto the deck. Mandy and Sandra were already there.

"Oh, Tom," Sandra said. "You should have seen Louis. As soon as he'd plugged back in his data boards, he wanted to get on with his observations. But even this little bit of rolling is ruining his measurements."

Mandy laughed. "You should have heard him, too. I learned some phrases we've never covered in Conversational French at Central Hills High."

"You can tell him that I'm going to try to fix things right now," Tom said. "Rick and I will be diving in a couple of minutes. We'll be carrying two hours of air, but expect us back in about half that time."

"Okay, Tom," Sandra said, checking her watch. "See you when you're through."

"One more thing," Tom said to his sister. He handed her the disk. "This contains a digitized picture from the underwater camera. Would you mind computer enhancing it? I'd like to see what it was that cut the line down there."

"No problem," Sandra said. "You guys have fun. I'll take care of this." She turned to Mandy. "Come on. As long as Louis can't do his experiments, maybe he'll let us have some time on his fancy computers."

Louis Armont had his laboratory down below on the second deck, all the way at the forward part of the platform. When Sandra and Mandy entered the compartment, he made a final note in the margin of the sheet of graph paper he was holding and looked up.

"Ah, young ladies," he said. "How may I assist you?"

"Well," Sandra said, "I was wondering if your computers are okay. Tom wants me to check out one of the pictures from that lost monitor camera."

"Of course my computers are okay," Louis responded with a twinkle in his eye. He nodded toward the console. "I learned how to secure for sea before your fathers were born. Trust me, if anything can come loose when the ocean becomes angry, it will. For this reason, I tie everything up or tie it down—and then do nothing to anger the sea."

Sandra sat down at the computer Louis had indicated, slipped the disk into the slot in its side, and called up a graphics program. Then she loaded the photographic image from the underwater monitor. The picture came up onto the screen one line at a time.

"What is it, do you think?" Mandy asked when the picture was fully displayed. "It's almost too blurry to make out anything at all."

"Let's try to bring it up," Sandra said.

She pushed a function button on the computer's console, and a menu labeled Enhance popped up on the screen. She selected Pixel Averaging from the list of options and pressed the Enter key. The image on the screen began to grow sharper.

"What's happening now?" Mandy asked.

"*Pixel* is short for 'picture element,'" Sandra explained. "Each of the dots on a computer screen—or on your TV screen at home—is a pixel. The computer gives each pixel a value for brightness, from 0 for dead black to 255 for pure white. And each dot has eight more dots around it, just like the squares on Louis's graph paper. So the computer finds the average brightness of the eight pixels bordering each dot on the screen. Then it changes the actual value of that center dot to the average value."

"How does that make the picture sharper?"

"It removes the random errors that give you fuzz and distortion," Sandra said. "One dot is more likely to have the wrong value than eight other dots are likely to be wrong. But the routine takes quite a while to run."

Soon enough, though, a clearer picture began to emerge on the screen.

"I do not believe," said Louis, "that it is a shark."

"No," Sandra said. Tom's sister began to feel a sinking sensation in her stomach, as if in foreboding of something unpleasant. "But maybe we can get it clearer."

While Mandy and Louis watched, she ran the next steps in the photo-enhancement process, this time using pattern-recognition and outline-determination software. Long before she was finished, however, the fate of the monitor camera had become obvious to the three of them.

The blurred shape in the original picture had taken on a solid form: a human hand and arm clad in a scuba diver's wet suit—the hand holding a pair of wire cutters.

4

As soon as Mandy and Sandra had gone below, Tom and Rick headed over to the floating habitat.

"We'll use the diving suits in here," Tom said.

"Those are the experimental suits, right?" Rick asked.

Tom nodded. "We can remove the debris and test the suits at the same time."

The two friends went into the habitat and took diving suits from the locker—a dark green one for Rick and a bright yellow one for Tom.

"This isn't like any other diving equipment you've ever used," Tom told his friend as they pulled on their suits. "It's made of a new synthetic substance I've developed, called baroplast. The more pressure you put on the suit's outer skin, the stronger it becomes. So the suits should be effectively pressure-proof."

Rick grinned. "Which means they'll also protect us against shark bites."

"That's right," said Tom. "Another reason for using these suits, just in case it really was one of Louis's big cable-eating sharks that got the monitor camera."

Tom shrugged on his suit's twin air tanks, then buckled on a belt filled with thirty pounds of lead weights. The belt also supported a container of dye marker to release into the water if the diver got into trouble. Another container held a Swift Enterprises inflatable life raft with emergency radio and radar beacon.

Rick fastened on his own belt at the same time. As he did so, he looked curiously at a pair of nozzles mounted on a swiveling base between the two air tanks on Tom's suit.

"What are the nozzles for?" Rick asked.

"They're a propulsion mechanism," Tom explained. "They take in water and force it out behind you in powerful streams. You can direct the jets to move yourself in any direction you choose."

Soon Tom and Rick had everything on except their swim fins and clear plastic helmets. Carrying the helmets and fins, they climbed back onto the floating platform.

"Ready to take the plunge?" Tom asked.

Rick nodded. "Ready."

"Then let's go." Tom pulled on his helmet. It snapped into place with a loud click. He turned the knob on his air tank and heard a soft hiss as the air mix began to flow. He took a deep breath, then let it out slowly.

He crouched on the edge of the platform and rolled off backward into the ocean. Jumping off might look flashier, but it could mean losing both air tanks from the impact. Then he was under the surface, tumbling wildly as a cloud of bubbles swirled around him. The bubbles cleared away, and he saw Rick treading water next to him.

The two teenage divers put on their swim fins. Then Tom lowered his chin and touched one of the small levers built into the fishbowllike plastic helmet.

"Rick," he said.

He saw Rick jerk in surprise as the words came to him inside his own helmet. Rick's lips moved soundlessly.

"I can't hear you," Tom said. "Touch your chest with your chin."

Rick bent his head. A second later, his puzzled voice came into Tom's helmet. "Tom? Can you hear me now? Something just went click."

"It's an underwater communications device," Tom said. "I call it an aqualingua. It uses infrared light instead of radio waves to carry signals back and forth, sort of like a cordless keyboard uses infrared light to send information to a computer. Just don't get more than fifty feet away from me, and stay in my line of sight."

"Sure," said Rick. "So what's first, now that we're down here?"

"That plastic sheet. Let's clear it away."

Tom and Rick spent half an hour clearing the plastic away from the hull. The sheet had stuck in place, sucked in by the water intakes and tangled among the vanes and stabilizers. Removing it was a ticklish job. They had to work carefully to avoid damaging the platform's delicate sensor equipment.

Tom put the freed pieces of plastic sheet on a hook lowered over the side of the platform. That way the scraps could be taken up on deck and disposed of properly.

"We still have half an hour before when we told Sandra we'd be back," Tom said to Rick after they'd finished. "So let's look for that monitor camera."

"Where?"

Tom pointed down toward the ocean's depths. "Down that way. Race you!"

By way of response, Rick turned head over heels in the water and began to swim toward the bottom. Tom paced him easily, glancing at his suit's depth gauge display projected in glowing numbers on the inside of his helmet. He and Rick were making good progress— they'd descended almost two hundred feet so far. The water around them grew darker until it seemed like perpetual twilight.

At this depth, Tom was glad they weren't wearing ordinary wet suits. If they had been, dissolved nitrogen from their air mix would already have begun to enter their blood. From there, the nitrogen might have formed bubbles in their joints, giving them a painful case of the bends or even killing them if they ascended too quickly. But Tom was confident that the constant pressure inside their baroplast suits would protect them.

After another hundred feet, the water was almost pitch-dark around them. Tom clicked on his suit's lights, using another chin switch.

"This is three hundred feet," he said. "I tested these suits in the pressure chamber at Swift Enterprises, so they should be safe to at least two thousand feet. The outer layer of the baroplast adjusts to the water's pressure, and the inner layer keeps a perfect one atmosphere of pressure inside the suit. We could probably go all the way down to the ocean floor and back up again without needing to worry."

"Maybe," said Rick. His voice sounded doubtful. "But have you noticed it's also getting harder to swim?"

Now that Rick mentioned the problem, Tom could feel that the outer skin of his suit had begun to stiffen on his body. A moment's thought gave him the explanation: As they descended, the water pressure against the suits constantly increased, and the baroplast responded by growing firmer and less flexible.

He relayed the explanation to Rick. "Our suits will become more rigid the deeper we go," he finished. "Eventually we won't be able to move our arms and legs at all. We'll have to use the jetpacks to maneuver."

"Sort of cuts down on what you can do underwater," Rick observed. "Think you can figure a way around the problem once you get back to the lab?"

"Give me a couple of weeks," Tom said. "I can imagine a couple of approaches that might work."

Rick chuckled. "And we'll need to field-test the suits again when they're completely finished. How about, say, in Hawaii?"

"Sounds good to me," said Tom. He activated his suit's jetpack with his chin.

When the jets were operating, a microcomputer built into the suit projected information onto the inside of Tom's helmet and also monitored where his eyes went. By adjusting the flow of water through the jets, the computer propelled Tom in the direction of his gaze. Using the jetpack, Tom could move through the water much faster than he could swim unaided. Tiny levers next to the aqualingua's controls allowed him to adjust the speed.

Rick had also turned on his jetpack by now, and the two friends jetted toward the ocean floor side by side. They played their lights ahead of them but couldn't see anything in the dark water below.

By five hundred feet, their suits had gone completely rigid. They couldn't move their arms and legs no matter how hard they tried. Using the jetpacks, they kept going down. Finally, at eight hundred and forty-five feet, they found the ocean floor.

The lights on their helmets shone onto sand and sediment that had been ridged and sculpted into soft dunes by water currents. Here and there gigantic rocks jutted up hundreds of feet. Where the bedrock had splintered and pulled apart, dark cracks extended thousands of feet into the seabed.

For a quarter of an hour, Tom and Rick prowled side by side through the surreal underwater landscape. "Time to go back," Rick said finally.

"Just a minute," Tom said, playing the beam of his light off to his left. "What's that over there?"

He jetted toward the dark shape that had drawn his attention—the looming hulk of a wrecked ship lying on its side. Tom guessed that in its day it had been nearly two hundred feet long. Now, however, worms and sea rot had eaten away its wooden deck, leaving only a rusted-out hull and scraps of iron. A huge, corroded anchor lay on the bottom some twenty feet away.

"How long do you think this thing has been here?" Rick asked, jetting up beside Tom. "Twenty years?"

"More," Tom said. He used his jets to propel himself up and over the top of the wreck. "Look how it's covered with a layer of sediment. Hey, what's this?"

On the far side of the ship, up against the remains of its hull, was a forty-foot-square tan-and-black mottled plastic tarp, pegged down to the sea floor with plastic stakes. Tom and Rick slowly jetted from left to right, playing their lights across the sheet's length. Whatever the tarp covered, it was big.

Tom swung down and awkwardly nudged up one edge of the tarp with his helmet. In his unbending suit, manipulating anything was next to impossible. His helmet light shone underneath the tarp, revealing dozens of black metal barrels lying on their sides and anchored to stakes in the seabed by yellow polypropylene line. Words had been stenciled in white on each barrel: Diesel Fuel Marine.

"This stuff can't be part of the wreck," Rick said, jetting up beside Tom. "I think somebody stashed it here. Fish don't use plastic camouflage sheets."

"I'd like to know who does, down here," said Tom.

"Uh-oh," Rick said, dropping his voice. "Someone's hiding down there with the barrels."

"Where?" Tom whispered back. Then he

laughed at himself. There was no reason to whisper. Unless the other diver also had an aqualingua, he couldn't hear anything.

Rick was still whispering, though. "Under the tarp."

"Okay," said Tom. "Here's what we'll do. You help me shove the tarp farther away from the barrels, and we'll find out if anybody's there. Remember, even if they turn out to be hostile, with the jetpacks we can head for the surface faster than anyone can swim. And *we* don't have to hang around partway up to decompress."

Without waiting for an answer, Tom began working his jets so that he could hook one arm underneath the tarp. Again the clumsiness of the maneuver made him frown. As soon as he got back to the Swift Enterprises labs, he decided, he'd see about fixing the suits' rigidity problem.

Once Rick also had an arm hooked beneath the tarp, Tom gave his friend a nod. "Now!" he said.

They jetted upward, pulling the tarp free of the stakes that had held it.

"There he is!" exclaimed Rick.

Tom glanced down. Sure enough, there was a diver, wearing a dive suit much like Tom's. Unlike the Swift Enterprises suits, however, his suit had a kind of heavy frame running along the diver's arms and legs. Tom tensed himself to jet for the surface as soon as the diver looked up and saw them.

Then he frowned. Something was wrong. The diver wasn't moving, only floating face-down a little above the bottom. Looking closer, Tom saw that a loop of the yellow line from one of the anchor stakes had become twisted around the mysterious diver's foot.

"Whoever that guy is," said Tom, "he can't work himself loose. We have to help him."

Tom jetted downward to float alongside the trapped diver. If the two of them put their helmets together, he thought, they should be able to talk even without an aqualingua. He gave the diver a push with his shoulder to attract his attention.

Propelled by the shove, the trapped diver turned slowly onto his back. Tom recoiled in surprise.

The diver's eyes were wide open and star-ing—and dead.

5

TOM LOOKED DOWN AT THE DEAD MAN.

"He couldn't get free," said Rick. "And then his air ran out. What a terrible way to die."

Tom had to agree. "We ought to get him loose and take him back to the surface," he said. "Maybe somebody on Bermuda will know who he is."

"Uh, yeah," Rick said after a minute. "But there's something else about that guy, isn't there. I mean, look at the insignia on his dive suit."

"I've been looking at it," said Tom. The unknown diver's suit was made of a black material similar to baroplast, surrounded by an external frame of heavy metal. The suit had a white circle emblazoned on the chest, and in the center of the circle was a stylized black dragon. "And I don't like it."

"I think I saw something like it at Lake Carlopa," Rick said. "But I don't know. . . ."

"Let's not fool ourselves," Tom said. "That dragon is the mark of Xavier Mace, one of the most brilliant, most twisted minds of the twentieth century. He'll do anything, anything at all, as long as he can see a profit for himself at the end of it. All he cares about is money. People mean less to him than the lab rats he uses in his experiments."

Rick laughed uneasily. "Come on, don't sugarcoat it. Tell me what you *really* think about the Black Dragon. But what's one of his people doing down here?"

"Whatever Mace is doing, it has to mean nothing good for us or for Bermuda." Tom sighed. "But that doesn't get us off the hook right now, though. We still have to get this man up to the platform."

Without being able to use their hands, however, Tom and Rick couldn't untie the line. And even with the aid of their jetpacks, the line around the diver's foot was too firmly tied and the stake too firmly in the seabed for them to pull the body free.

"Okay," said Tom finally. "Let's get out of here." Then he paused. "Wait a minute. Either I'm seeing things or something is showing a light behind that rise in the seabed over there to the south."

"If you're crazy, Tom, so am I," said Rick,

"because I see it, too. Whatever it is, there's a bunch of them, and they're coming closer."

"Quick!" Tom said. "We have to kill our lights right now, before they spot us."

They turned off their suit lights and floated silently in the dark water, watching.

As the bobbing lights came nearer, Tom saw that there were five of them, each attached to the airpack on the back of a diving suit. The newcomers all wore black diving suits like that of the dead man, with the heavy external frames and the dragon symbol emblazoned on the chest. The divers swam freely, and Tom realized that the frames must be mechanical exoskeletons allowing them to move their arms and legs despite the stiffness of their suits under pressure.

"Jet back slowly," Tom said to Rick over the aqualingua. "Go behind the ship where they can't see us."

The two of them jetted as carefully as they could around the tarp covering the oil drums and from there into the shelter of the ship's rusted-out hull. From that vantage point they watched as the five divers, each carrying a spear gun and a knife, swam up to the hidden oil drums where the dead man floated silent and still.

One of the divers drew his knife from his belt and slashed the entangling line. Then two of the other divers grabbed the dead man under his armpits and began hauling him back the way they'd come.

"Looks like that guy's buddies came to his rescue a bit too late," Tom said as the divers' lights vanished into the blackness. "Time to get out of here."

"For once, I totally agree," Rick said.

Turning on their helmet lights again, they jetted away from the sunken ship and up toward the surface.

The water grew steadily brighter, until suddenly they could make out the shifting, light-spangled surface of the water and the immense black rectangle of the oceangoing platform floating overhead. But even as Tom swam the last few feet to the surface, his thoughts kept turning to the image of a dead man in a dive suit marked with the emblem of the Black Dragon.

Up on the floating platform, Sandra Swift was getting worried. For the last half hour, she had been waiting on deck near the place where Tom and Rick had submerged. Now she turned away from the sea and went into the pilothouse, where Captain O'Brien was working with his charts.

"Tom said he'd be back in an hour," Sandra told O'Brien. "That was an hour and a half ago. He has only thirty minutes of air left. And we have this." She waved the computer-enhanced photo. "I'm sure Tom's in trouble."

"I don't like it, either," O'Brien said. "I promised your father that I'd take care of you. Losing Tom isn't what he had in mind, I'm sure."

Just then a shout sounded from outside. "I see them!"

It was Mandy. "Tom and Rick are back," she called up to the pilothouse. "They're changing out of their diving suits right now, and they say they have something to report. They think what happened to us was sabotage."

"Well, they're right about that," O'Brien commented to Sandra. "I think it's about time we discussed what's happened since noon today." He shook his head. "Sandra, go and tell the others that we're having a meeting in the crew's mess in five minutes."

Sandra went down to the main deck of the platform, out where the habitat was tied up. Tom and Rick were just coming back from stowing their dive suits.

"What kept you guys?" Sandra asked them. "You'd better hurry—Captain O'Brien has called a meeting."

Rick's usually cheerful features looked grim. "Tom can tell everyone the whole story then," he said. "But here's the short version: We found a dead man on the bottom of the ocean. And that's the *good* news."

*   *   *

The crew's mess on the oceangoing platform was a comfortable compartment along
the centerline, just aft of the ladder. It had
genuine portholes spaced along the bulkhead,
their heavy glass surrounded by polished
brass and, for a homey touch, lace curtains.
A snug galley lay outboard of the mess on the
port side. When Tom and the others entered,
Louis Armont was just emerging from the galley with a steaming mug of coffee in his hand.

The oceanographer shook his head ruefully
as he went over to sit beside Matt and Bob
Weinberg. "What a disaster," Louis said. "Our
adventures of this afternoon have left us without a single unbroken egg on board. How
shall I make my omelet tomorrow morning?"

Tom couldn't help chuckling. Louis was
serious about only two things in life—the
health of the world's oceans and his breakfast.

A moment later O'Brien walked in and
glanced around. "Let's see," he said. "Dr.
Armont, I see your team is here. Tom, you
and your friends are here. And I've put my
four sailors on watch, so everyone on board
is either present or accounted for."

O'Brien walked into the galley to draw
himself a cup of coffee, continuing to talk as
he did so. "I've reported today's events to Mr.
Swift via communications satellite," he said.
"The message I received back was 'Use your
discretion. Keep me advised.' "

He reentered the mess and sat at the table,

cradling a coffee mug in his hand. "What do we know so far?"

Tom's sister was the first to speak. "The loss of the monitor camera was deliberate sabotage," Sandra said as she laid the photo on the table. "There's no way a cut cable and a diver with a wire cutter could be coincidence."

"Which implies that the plastic on our intakes was no coincidence, either," O'Brien said.

"One thing that disturbs me," said Bob Weinberg, "is that if Captain O'Brien hadn't gotten the malfunctioning stabilizers shut down in time, we might have been just another mysterious disappearance in the Bermuda Triangle. Whoever performed this sabotage must have had a good idea what the effect on the platform would be."

Tom cleared his throat. "I think I know who that someone is," he said, then told the others what he and Rick had seen down on the ocean floor.

"The Black Dragon," said Louis Armont. "I have heard of him. He is one of the true enemies of the earth."

"We don't like him much at Swift Enterprises, either," O'Brien said. "Any theories about what he's doing here?"

"After what Tom did to him at Lake Carlopa, blowing up his entire factory complex there, he might try to sink us just to get Tom," Rick suggested.

"Thanks for the cheerful thought," Tom said. "But if he just wanted to get me, he wouldn't need things like submerged fuel dumps."

"How about all those other missing ships?" Mandy asked hesitantly. "When did those start?"

"In the Triangle?" said O'Brien. "Centuries ago."

"No, no," Mandy said. "You told us earlier today that this has been an especially bad year for missing ships. Well, I think Xavier Mace has been at work here for a long time. There's no way he could have known when he started that Tom was going to be on the platform."

"You've got a point," admitted O'Brien. "But what is there about the ocean in this area to attract Mace?"

Tom looked over at Louis. "You're the expert. Is there anything unusual in the waters around Bermuda?"

"Bermuda is a mysterious place," Louis began, "hundreds of miles from the nearest land, unique. Why is it here? I had no answer, and for that reason, I began my research. I believe that I have found something about Bermuda that no one has previously suspected."

The Frenchman looked at Matt Weinberg. "Would you fetch my charts, please, Matt?"

As the younger geophysicist left, Louis continued, "I assume you know about the theory of plate tectonics. To be brief, according to this theory, the continents as we know them are part of vast plates floating on the surface of the world much as icebergs float on the surface of the sea. When the plates press against one another, the result is a mountain range, and when they rub past each other, the result is an earthquake. Do you follow so far?"

The others nodded.

"Very good. There are a number of such plates. You may have noticed that the west coast of Africa roughly matches the east coast of South America. One coast represents the African Plate, the other the South American Plate. These plates have been drifting apart for millions of years. Under the Pacific, to the north of South America, the Cocos Plate presses against the Caribbean Plate from the west, thrusting up the mountains of Central America. Where the Caribbean Plate presses against the North American Plate, voilà—we find Cuba, Hispaniola, Puerto Rico, and the Leeward and Windward Islands."

Louis broke off as Matt Weinberg reappeared, carrying a sheaf of rolled-up charts.

"Thank you, Matt," Louis said. The Frenchman looked through the collection of charts, selected one, and spread it out on the mess table.

"Some of these tectonic plates are much smaller. For example, there is the Caroline Plate, containing the Caroline Islands in the Pacific, and the Fiji Plate, which contains Fiji alone. But I believe that here beneath the ocean around Bermuda I have discovered yet another tectonic plate, the smallest so far detected."

Louis pointed to the lines he had drawn on his chart. "All the measurements I have made so far—measurements more detailed than any previously possible, thanks to this excellent platform—tell me that the island of Bermuda rests on a microplate all of its own."

Rick shook his head. "That's it?" he asked. "No undersea oil wells? No lumps of gold lying around on the bottom? Why should the Black Dragon care about an accident of geology?"

Tom looked again at the markings on the chart. He couldn't imagine what an obscure discovery like the Bermuda microplate might suggest to a criminal genius. But he felt sure Mace was up to something.

"If I know the Black Dragon," Tom said slowly, "we won't be curious for long. He's already attacked us once unsuccessfully, and Xavier Mace is not the sort of man who deals well with failure."

6

W<small>E OUGHT TO REPORT THIS TO THE AUTHORI</small>-ties on Bermuda," Mandy said. "Trying to sink someone is probably all kinds of illegal."

"I suppose," Tom replied. "But there are still things we don't know, like what Mace is doing with the ships he's taking, if he's taking them at all."

"The sunken ships are speculation," said O'Brien. "But the attempted sabotage—now, that's a fact. Mandy's right—it ought to be reported."

"Then we should go to Bermuda to make our report in person," said Tom. "Using the radio might not be safe if the Black Dragon is listening in."

Captain O'Brien looked at the clock mounted on the bulkhead. "Well, it's after fifteen hundred now—that's three P.M., to you—and we're forty miles east of Saint George, Bermuda. The utility boat makes only twenty knots, so you'd better leave right now if you're planning to reach land before sunset."

"Right," Tom said. He turned to his sister. "If I'm going in, Sandra, I'll need that photo of yours."

Sandra shook her head. "Oh, no. You aren't going to hit the beaches of Bermuda without me."

"Or me," Mandy added. "I've been waiting for a chance to go sightseeing."

"Right," Captain O'Brien said. "Why don't you all go? I'll send Booth and Jones with you. They have a list of spares and replacements to pick up in Hamilton, anyway. Try to be back by midnight."

Tom and his friends left the mess and went up to the main deck. There they were joined by Lloyd Jones—a thin, laconic man in his early thirties—and by Katie Booth. Katie had a rolled-up chart and a logbook tucked under her arm.

"You guys ready?" Jones asked the teenagers. "Then let's go."

Katie laughed. "But don't blame us if the island's not as lively as you expected it to be. Take it from me, about the most exciting thing you can do on Bermuda is stand around and watch the seagulls yawn."

They walked over to the utility boat, slung from davits amidships on the platform's starboard side. "Good thing you didn't get smashed by the sea this afternoon," Jones said to the boat as he loosened the grips holding it in place, "or we wouldn't be going anywhere."

Jones swung the boat out on its davits and lowered it until its gunwale was even with the edge of the deck.

"All aboard that's coming," he said.

The others climbed over the rail into the boat, where they put on the life jackets that were stowed in the bilges. Katie Booth picked up the radio handset and keyed the mike.

"Tango Sierra," she said, using the call sign of the floating platform. "This is Tango Sierra One. Radio check, over."

"This is Tango Sierra," the radio crackled in O'Brien's voice. "Roger, over."

"This is Tango Sierra One, roger, out," Katie said, and put down the handset.

Once everybody was jacketed and seated, Jones continued lowering the boat until it was just above the water. "Fire it up," he called down to Katie. She pushed the autostarter on the control panel and was rewarded with a roar from the engine. Jones finished lowering the boat into the water, then climbed hand over hand down a line to join the others. Soon they were heading away from the side of the platform and out into the sea, deep blue and clear.

"Okay," Katie said, "who wants to steer first?"

Rick was the first to answer. "I will," he said.

"Right," said Katie. "Just watch the compass needle and keep it on two-seven-three. If the needle swings right, you put on right rudder till it gets back. The needle swings left, you put on left rudder."

Rick took the wheel, and Katie moved aside to stand at his shoulder in the coxswain's position. "Under way at fifteen-oh-three local time from the Swift floating platform, bound for Saint George, Bermuda," she muttered while writing in the logbook. "Setting course two-seven-three per magnetic compass, making turns for twenty knots. Okay, people—our first sight of land should be Saint David's Light, dead ahead at around sixteen hundred hours. Keep a sharp watch."

On the floating platform, Captain O'Brien watched the small boat depart, following it with binoculars until it was over the horizon.

Louis Armont came onto the bridge to stand beside him. "Is there anything that I can do?" the Frenchman asked.

"I don't know," O'Brien replied. "It looks like we may have a whole bunch of unfriendly divers under us. I'd like to keep them from trying to sink us again. Next time they might forget about playing cute tricks with plastic sheeting and just bring along a couple of five-pound demolition blocks. That would ruin my whole day."

"Of a certainty, it would do so," agreed Louis. "How, then, are you planning to stop them?"

"I think I'm going to go active on sonar," O'Brien said after a moment's thought. "I haven't done that yet, to keep from messing up your experiments. But I'm the captain, and right now in my judgment maintaining the safety of the platform outranks collecting data."

"You will hear no arguments from me," Louis assured him. "My instruments and I can collect our data another time, but not if we go down to the bottom of the ocean together and do not come up again."

"Glad you agree," said O'Brien. "The sonar will give us plenty of warning if more unfriendlies show up." He grinned. "Another good thing—with all the wattage we'll be putting into the water, they won't be able to get *too* close unless they want some world-class headaches."

He switched on a panel on the bridge. "Here," he said to Louis. "If you still want to help out while your own instruments are down, you can watch this screen. If you see any blips on it, let me know."

The screen was circular and glowed with green light. Suddenly a high-pitched four-note sequence sounded, seeming to come from everywhere at once. "That's the first ping," O'Brien said. "Now watch."

Louis chuckled. "Ah, *mon capitaine*," he said as a ring of light bloomed from the center of the screen and expanded toward its edge. Some tiny dots of light remained. One dot, at the bottom of the screen, stayed bright longer than the rest. "I was not born yesterday. You do not have to explain the display of a sonar screen to me. That was an echo from something in the water, just before the bottom return."

The tone sequence sounded again. Another ring of light rushed outward from the center of the display. Once more the bright dot appeared, this time to the right of where its first mark was fading from the screen.

"You've got it," O'Brien said. "And see how far it's moved. Whoever or whatever it is, it's going pretty fast."

A third ping, and the blip no longer painted the screen. O'Brien shook his head.

"Whatever it was, it's gone now. But that's what we're looking for. Anything like that shows up, I want to know about it. I know a couple of tricks, and anyone who wants to sink me had better want to *real* bad."

The captain left the bridge. Louis Armont settled down to watch the screen as yet another ping filled the air and the sea around him.

* * *

In the utility boat, Tom now had the helm. Mandy Coster was sitting beside him.

"I know there's no proof," she said, "but I can't help thinking that what Louis found out about the ocean floor is related to what the Black Dragon is doing."

"Me, too," Tom said. "But I can't for the life of me figure out what it is. Do you have any suggestions?"

Mandy shook her head. "No. What are you going to tell the police when we get to Bermuda?"

"The Bermuda police don't have jurisdiction out at sea," Tom said. "I'm going straight to the United States Naval Air Station."

"Hey, look!" Rick shouted. "Uh, I mean, land ho!"

"Land aye," Katie Booth replied, stifling a laugh. "Looks like Saint David's, all right, two points on the port bow. Tom, come left."

Tom put on left rudder. When the bow of the utility boat was pointed directly at the top of the lighthouse, just visible above the waves on the horizon, Katie called out, "Steady as you go."

The utility boat cruised onward. Soon the pink limestone houses of Saint David's Island rose up above the sea ahead, their white roofs dazzling in the late afternoon sun. Beyond them, in the distance, Tom could see the green hills of Great Bermuda Island.

He drew in a deep breath. Even out here on

the water, he could smell a change in the air. Instead of smelling clear and salty, it smelled sweet, like flowers, with a bit of the spicy tang of citrus.

"Mmm," said Mandy a moment later. "Where did the perfume come from all of a sudden?"

"That's Bermuda itself you're smelling," Katie Booth told them. "There aren't enough cars on the island to stink up the air with their exhaust, and you don't get stuff rotting in the heat and wet as you do closer to the equator. When the wind's right, you can smell the flowers of Bermuda a long time before you get there."

The sun was close to the horizon by the time they tied up at the Yacht Club mooring in Saint George's harbor. "It's getting late," Tom said. "Rick and I had better hit the naval air station while the rest of you pick up supplies."

Katie Booth looked at her watch. "It's seventeen hundred now, so let's meet here at twenty-one thirty. That should get us back to the platform by midnight."

The group split up. Tom and Rick took a cab west along Wellington Street, then over the Severn Bridge to the island of Saint David's. The driver came to a halt outside the gate of the naval air station.

"Sorry, but this is as far as I can take you."

"Don't worry about it," Tom replied as he paid the fare. "This'll do."

A young marine in dress blues stood inside the whitewashed concrete guardhouse. "Good afternoon, gentlemen," she said when Tom and Rick walked up to the gate. "May I be of assistance?"

"Yes," Tom replied. "I'm an American citizen, and I'd like to speak with whoever is in charge."

"One moment," she replied. "I'll call the sergeant of the guard."

She spoke briefly over the guardhouse telephone. In a couple of minutes a white pickup truck with navy stencils on the doors drove up from somewhere inside the air station. The driver was another young marine.

"You guys the civilians who want to see the command duty officer?" he asked. They nodded. "Okay," the marine replied, "jump in."

Tom and Rick climbed into the front seat of the pickup for another short ride. The sun was starting to go down in a brilliant display of orange and black as they halted outside a white-painted building. The United States flag was flying from the flagpole out front.

"I'll take you in through the quarterdeck," the marine driver said. He led Tom and Rick into the building.

Inside, pictures of the air station's officers, the president of the United States, and assorted naval aircraft lined the walls. Nearby, an American flag and a navy flag stood together in a small roped-off area. Above a nearby office door was a sign in white letters on black plastic: Command Duty Officer.

The driver ushered Tom and Rick through the door. A man in a khaki uniform with gold oak leaves pinned to his collar sat behind the room's only desk, a clipboard full of papers in his hand. On the wall behind him hung a map of Bermuda. The officer stood when the boys entered.

"Good evening, gentlemen," he said. "I'm Lieutenant Commander Otano. How can I help you?"

"I'm Thomas Swift, Jr.," Tom said. "I'm working on an experimental floating platform about forty miles east of here. I think someone is trying to sink us."

"Are you sure? That's a pretty serious allegation." Lieutenant Commander Otano sat down again and pulled a pad of paper out of the center drawer of the desk. He picked up a black ballpoint pen and clicked it open. "Okay, why don't you tell me the whole story from the beginning?"

Together, Tom and Rick told Lieutenant Commander Otano about the plastic sheet on the floating platform, the photograph of the hand with the wire cutter, and the divers on the sea floor. Watching the officer's face, Tom was glad that he'd brought along Sandra's digitized picture to back up his story. It would give the navy something to go on besides his word alone.

When Tom had finished, Lieutenant Commander Otano looked at him with a serious expression. "You mentioned someone you think is behind all this. Could you tell me the name again?"

"Sure," said Tom. "The dead diver and his buddies were all wearing a symbol that's associated with Xavier Mace, also known as the Black Dragon."

Otano nodded. "That's what I thought you said. Would you excuse me for a minute?"

The officer picked up the telephone on his desk and dialed a number. "Hello, Sam? Andres here. Yeah, I have the duty tonight. Listen, a couple of civilians came in a few minutes ago and told me an interesting story. No, I'm not going to tell you on the phone—this isn't a secure line. I'm down at HQ. Could you come over? I think you want to hear this. See you in a couple of minutes."

Lieutenant Commander Otano put the receiver back onto its cradle. "Okay, guys," he said to Tom and Rick. "I sure hope you two aren't making all this up because our intelligence officer is on his way over right now."

7

LIEUTENANT COMMANDER OTANO LOOKED AT Tom and Rick gravely. "When Sam gets here, I want you to tell him the same story that you told me. Normally, I'd just put all this into a situation report and pass it on up the line. But when you mention the Black Dragon, you're talking about somebody the federal government has what you might call a continuing interest in. So I sure hope you aren't making this up."

"Honest, sir," said Tom. "We aren't messing around."

"I believe you, actually," Otano replied. "I had to warn you, though, just to have that on the record. But everybody's heard of Tom Swift. We use stuff that was either designed or built by Swift Enterprises ourselves."

At that moment another khaki-clad man walked in. "Hi, Andres," he said. "These the civilians?"

"Yeah," Otano said. "I'd like you to meet Tom Swift and Rick Cantwell. Tom, Rick, this is Lieutenant Commander Pena. Sam, these young men have been having adventures east of here. Check out this photo."

Otano handed the picture of the diver's hand with the wire cutters to the intelligence officer. Pena looked over the picture.

"Interesting," he said. "This is a computer enhancement. You don't happen to have the original picture, do you?"

Tom shook his head. "I'm afraid not. The original was pretty blurry."

"Too bad," Pena said. "Can I keep this one, then?"

"Sure," Tom said.

"Fine. Now tell me the story that goes with it."

For the third time that day, Tom found himself telling the story of the attempted sabotage, the missing camera, and the dead diver with the Black Dragon's logo on his chest.

When Tom was done, Otano looked over at Pena. "I told you it was interesting, didn't I?"

"Yeah," Pena said. He turned back to Tom. "Listen, is there any way for you and your people to clear out of that general area? The reason I'm asking is, if you really have this certain individual out there, you probably shouldn't mess with him. Criminals, terrorists . . . well, they're hard to predict. And this one's a nasty customer."

"We know that already," Tom said. "But we're a legitimate research operation, and I don't want to get shut down just because a 'certain individual' is alive somewhere on earth."

Pena shrugged. "Any way you want to play it," he said. "Just wanted to make sure you guys knew what you were walking into. Now, here's the way it is: You and Xavier Mace are both in international waters. The United States government has no jurisdiction there. The Bermudan government has no jurisdiction there, either. So as long as Mace isn't violating international law, he's got as much right to operate there as you have."

Rick flushed an indignant red. "But—" he started to say.

Pena held up a hand and went on. "You suspect and I suspect that Mace is up to no good. And personally, I would bet my paycheck that he destroyed your camera and tried to sink your platform. But without proof, your suspicions and mine won't hold up in an Admiralty Court. Now, if Mace were performing acts of piracy or something like that . . ."

"How about all those ships he's been sinking?" Rick persisted.

Pena shook his head. "I'm sorry," he said. "We don't *know* that he's been sinking anybody. All we have is a collection of missing ships, and vessels have been turning up missing in these waters for hundreds of years. The entire thing stinks, I agree, but we still don't have enough to go on. The best I can do is pass the report up my chain of command. Maybe they can put it together with some other information that I don't have and make a case."

"I understand," said Tom, although he couldn't help feeling disappointed.

Lieutenant Commander Otano caught his expression. "There is one other thing we can do," Otano said. "We fly regular antisubmarine warfare patrols out of here, P-3 Orions covering the Greenland–Iceland–United Kingdom gap. I can alter the flight paths to overfly your position and tell the pilots to keep an eye out for any unusual activities. If we spot anything, we'll let you know. And if anything involving the Black Dragon comes up from your side, you let us know, okay? We have helicopters here. If things get too messy, we can put a squad of combat-ready marines on your deck in twenty minutes."

"I understand," Tom said.

"That's about it, guys," Pena added. "Until we have a major crime under international law, there's not much else we can do. Remember, my official recommendation is that you clear the area right now."

"Thanks," Tom said. "I'll pass that along to Captain O'Brien." Then he had an idea.

"There is one more thing, if it's okay with you—"

"What's that?" asked Otano curiously.

"Well, if it isn't classified information, could I have a list of all the ships reported missing in this area over the last year?"

"Sure," Otano said. "That's a matter of public record." He pulled a clipboard down from the wall and handed it across the desk to Tom. "Here they are. Copy 'em down if you want."

It was late evening by the time Tom and Rick returned to King's Square. A few of the brighter stars already showed against the sky overhead, their glow softened a little by the humidity. Mandy and Sandra were waiting for the boys when they arrived.

"Where are Jones and Katie?" Tom asked.

"They took the boat around to Hamilton to load supplies," Sandra replied. "They said they'd meet us at the dock at nine-thirty."

"That gives us a couple of hours to kill," said Tom. "What do you want to do?"

"I don't know about the rest of you," Rick said, "but I want to eat. That roller-coaster ride we went on at noon kept us from having lunch, and I haven't had a chance to grab anything more than a snack since."

Eventually the four teenagers wound up at a small restaurant called the White Horse on Saint David's Island. There they sat at a picnic table outdoors, looking over the menu of Bermudan specialties with curious eyes.

" 'Curried conch stew,' " Sandra read. "That sounds like it might not be too bad. I'll give it a try."

"I'm going for mussels and rice," Mandy decided. "How about you, Tom? Doesn't anybody want to live dangerously and try the shark hash?"

Tom shook his head. "Sorry. I was thinking of finding out if the spiny lobster is in season right now. If anybody gets the hash, it'll have to be Rick."

"Sure," said Rick. "Eat the shark before he eats you. I'll take my chances on the hash, and Tom can order all the lobster he wants."

When the waiter showed up to take their orders, however, both the spiny lobster and the shark hash turned out to be unavailable, much to Rick's disappointment.

"Now what am I going to do?" he asked. "I was all set to tell the gang back at Central Hills about the time I put the bite on a shark."

The waiter looked sympathetic. "The availability of different items varies, especially when you buy or catch everything fresh each day as we do. Lately the availability's mostly been going down, I'm afraid. The fishing boats aren't bringing in as much as usual."

Something in the waiter's voice stirred Tom's curiosity. "Have the fishing boats been having some sort of trouble?" he asked. "Anything that might account for the catch being smaller?"

The waiter shook his head. "Mostly the fish just aren't there. But there have been a few wild stories making the rounds. Some of the fishing crews claim a sea monster is scaring off the fish, but that's just talk. Nobody really believes them."

"What sort of sea monster?" Tom asked.

The waiter shrugged. "The sort you find at the bottom of a bottle, if you ask me. 'Big as a mountain, green eyes glowing in the dark'— that kind of thing."

"Sounds a lot like bad special effects," commented Tom. "Where do the boat crews claim to have been fishing when they've spotted this monster?"

"East of here, usually," the waiter told him. "That's where the best fishing used to be."

"About how far east, do you know?"

"Oh, twenty to forty miles offshore," said the waiter. "Sometimes more, sometimes less."

"Interesting," said Tom. He pulled out the list of missing ships he'd copied down at the naval air station and scribbled a note at the bottom of the page. "*Very* interesting."

The sun was setting over the Swift Enterprises floating platform. Louis Armont remained on the bridge, watching the sonar display. The screen was still blank except for the expanding rings of green lights that etched their way across the field with every ping.

Nothing had returned to the scope since the first two blips on the screen had vanished, but Louis had many years of experience in persuading the ocean to give up its secrets and had learned how to wait. He watched the screen patiently. Behind him the voice of the weather radio whispered away, reading the predictions for the northern Atlantic over and over again.

Captain O'Brien climbed up the ladder from the main deck, carrying a couple of cans of soft drinks. "Here," he said, passing one of the cans across to Louis. "And thanks for holding down the sonar. The last few hours have probably been pretty boring."

Louis accepted the can with a smile. "When I was young," he said, "I might have felt as you say. In those days, yes, I ran away from boredom the way less foolhardy men ran away from trouble. But now I am older, and I hope a little wiser, and I know that boredom is very much preferable to what might otherwise be happening."

"You've got that right," said O'Brien. "Right now my sense of adventure is packed somewhere down at the bottom of my seabag. Oh, well, time to observe sunset."

The captain turned on the platform's aircraft warning lights, its running lights, and the red-over-white-over-red lights warning other ships that his vessel was restricted in its ability to maneuver. Then he sat down in a swivel chair bolted to the deck of the pilothouse.

"So," he said to Louis after a while. "Do you and the Weinbergs have any ideas about what Mace might be up to?"

The Frenchman shook his head. "I am afraid, no. If we had not just begun to take measurements of this portion of the Bermuda Plate ... But our maps for this last area remain incomplete. If the Black Dragon was here before us, then he may know something that we do not."

"That's what I figured," said O'Brien as another ping sent an expanding ring out onto the screen. "So all we can do is wait for him to make trouble. Maybe it would be better to break off the expedition early and head back to Cape Hatteras in the morning."

He frowned out at the sunset. "But just between you and me, Armont, I hate letting that villain scare us off."

"As do I, *mon capitaine*. But you are responsible for the platform and for the lives aboard—"

Louis broke off in midsentence. "Listen! I believe the weather radio is saying something about Bermuda."

O'Brien nodded. "I caught it," he said. "Small craft advisories for the Bermuda area."

The captain walked out onto the bridge

wing and looked briefly at the sky. Then he came back onto the bridge and checked the barometer.

"The air pressure's fallen, all right," he said. "There's bad weather coming."

Conversation lagged, and eventually the two men sat without speaking, listening to the steady voice of the weather radio and the regular pinging of the sonar. Outside, the sunset over Bermuda gradually darkened into night. Then it began to grow darker still, as storm clouds from the south blew up and raced across the sky, eating the stars as they came.

8

TOM SWIFT HELD ON TIGHT AS A WAVE CRASHED over the bow of the utility boat. Spray flew, and rain poured down from the dark sky overhead.

The boat pitched steeply up one side of a wave, then slid down the other. The storm had blown up not long after the utility boat had pulled away from the pier at Saint George's, and everybody on board was soaked to the skin.

Katie Booth, the most experienced sailor on board, had the wheel and was fighting the seas to keep the boat on course. Tom, with Lloyd Jones, was standing by at the engine, ready to go to work if it should die and need to be restarted.

"How long have we been under way?" Rick shouted from where he sat with Sandra and Mandy amid the crates and bags of supplies.

73

Tom could barely hear his friend's voice over the sound of the wind and the roar of the utility boat's engine running flat out.

"An hour and a half," Tom shouted back, after a glance at the red numbers on his chronolaser. "We should have the platform in sight by now."

"I don't see it. Do you see it?"

"No," said Tom. "Katie! Do you know where the platform is?"

"No," she called back. "I expect we've been set to the north by the wind. At two hours out, we'll turn south and see if we can locate it."

Another wave dumped water over the gunwales of the utility boat. The bilge pumps, running continuously now, emptied it back over the side again.

"Can I use the radio?" Tom asked.

"Go for it. I've got my hands full."

Tom scrambled over and picked up the radio handset. "Tango Sierra," he called, "this is Tango Sierra One. Interrogative, do you hold me on radar, over."

The radio receiver on the utility boat crackled into life. "Tango Sierra One, this is Tango Sierra. Negative, I say again negative, over."

"Tango Sierra One, roger, out." Tom put down the handset. "The platform doesn't have us on the scope."

"Not surprising," Katie said. "We're probably lost in the sea return. The waves are higher than we are."

Her words gave Tom an idea. "Hang on," he said. "I have something that may work." He turned his wrist so that the chronolaser pointed straight up. "Okay, everybody, watch your eyes."

He moved his fingers in the coded pattern that would activate the chronolaser's cutting function. A beam of light strong enough to cut metal burned skyward, visible where the rain and spray scattered it as it ascended. He kept the beam pointed up and reached for the radio handset with his other hand.

"Tango Sierra," he said, "this is Tango Sierra One. I am showing a red light. Interrogative, do you have me on visual, over."

"This is Tango Sierra, wait, out."

A moment passed and another. The red beam shone upward into the storm-wracked sky. The radio crackled again. "Tango Sierra One, this is Tango Sierra. I hold a column of red light bearing zero-two-three true, over."

Tom gave a sigh of relief. "This is Tango Sierra One, that's me, out." He put down the handset and turned off the chronolaser's beam. "Okay, Katie, you got it."

"Beats shooting off a signal flare," she said. "We bear zero-two-three from them, so they must bear two-zero-three from us."

She put the wheel hard right and came sharply about. The ride became even wilder now, with the waves hitting them directly on the bow. The boat was constantly surging and pounding, going up over the crest of a wave and down into the trough, only to rise on the next wave.

They were riding high on the crest of a particularly big wave, hanging there in the instant before slamming down into the trough, when Mandy called out, "There's a light ahead! It's the platform!"

With the lights of the floating platform to guide them, the rest of the ride, while still rough, was at least short. Soon the boat was once more tied up alongside the platform. Captain O'Brien had brought the automatic stabilizers back on-line. In contrast to the violent motion of the sea, the deck of the platform remained as steady as Bermuda itself.

"Well," Tom said when they all finally stood on the deck, "this is another test we needed to make, to see how the platform held up in a storm."

"Are you sure it's doing all that well?" Rick asked. "It looks steady, but I can feel it moving."

"We're steady, all right," Tom answered. "You just haven't gotten your land legs back after that boat ride."

He led the way back onto the bridge. There he found Louis Armont sitting in front of the sonar scope and Captain O'Brien waiting, as well.

"How did it go on shore?" O'Brien asked.

"Only so-so," admitted Tom. "We did get the names of all the ships that have vanished recently, and we found out that the Black Dragon is known to the authorities. But no one can do anything unless he tries something obvious. We've got the promise of help if we need it, and if the navy spots anything unusual on their regular patrols, they'll let us know."

"That's not good enough," said O'Brien, frowning. "It's not our job to play bait for an international terrorist. I'm using that authority your father gave me and cutting the expedition short. We're heading back toward Hatteras tomorrow morning."

"It cannot be helped, I suppose," said Louis. "Bob and Matt will not be very happy, but there is always another time."

"For you, maybe," said Tom. "But this means that if I'm going to bring home any more information about what the Black Dragon is up to, I'll have to get it tonight."

"At midnight in this weather?" said Rick. "You're crazy, do you know that? Why don't you stay on board and get some sleep?"

"I can sleep tomorrow while the platform's heading back home," Tom said. "And the storm's at the top of the ocean, not the bottom. But since today's already been a long day, I won't dive. I'll play it safe and take the minisub down."

"The sub is a two-seater," Sandra said. "You'll need someone else along who's also fully qualified to run it."

"Are you saying that you want to come?" Tom asked.

"Why should you and Rick have all the fun?" she replied. "Let's go."

Tom pulled his notes out of his pocket. The ride back in the utility boat had left them somewhat damp but still legible. "We'll launch the sub right after I transmit the names of these missing ships to Dad. Maybe he can find something they all have in common."

As soon as the transmission was completed, Tom and Sandra went back down to the main deck. There the wind tugged at their clothes, and the driving rain plastered their hair to their heads.

"Let's go to the habitat and put on our dive suits first," Tom said. "Just in case we have to leave the sub."

"Good idea," Sandra said.

Inside the floating habitat, Tom and his sister suited up quickly by the dim red glow of the emergency lights. Tom once again wore his bright yellow suit, and Sandra chose a red one.

"There's one thing I found out today," Tom said. "The baroplast stiffens as you go deeper. If you have to use the suit, try not to go below about three hundred feet."

They reemerged from the habitat with the

globular dive helmets tucked under their arms. Flippers in hand, they walked across the gangplank to the main deck, where the mini-sub lay waiting in its hidden berth.

Tom knelt and flipped open a control panel set into the deck. "Swift," he said into the panel's microphone. The computer checked his voiceprint against its records in a fraction of a second.

"Approved," it said in a metallic voice.

"Open sesame," Tom said.

Metal plates clanked and groaned as a ten-by-four-foot section of the deck slid back to reveal the minisub. The submersible looked more like a short, squat missile than anything else, a stubby cylinder painted in blue-and-green undersea camouflage patterns. A rounded nose tapered back to the fins and to the jets in the rear. Tom opened the hatch and climbed in, with Sandra following close behind.

He pulled the hatch closed and sealed it. Inside, the minisub held enough equipment to keep even Louis Armont and the Weinbergs happy: sonar screens, radar scopes, radio sets, computer consoles, and more gauges, read-outs, dials, and switches than Tom could count in one glance. Everything was crammed into a space barely large enough for two people. Tom squeezed into one of the tiny seats, and Sandra took the other, sitting behind him and facing the opposite direction.

Tom set the helmet of his dive suit on his lap and pulled the sub's viewscope down into position in front of his eyes. With the sub still inside its holding bay, all he could see was a closeup of some metal panels.

"Ready, Sandra?" he asked.

"Ready."

Tom started running down the predive checklist. "All equipment secured?"

"Check," Sandra answered.

"Ports cleared?"

"Check."

"Ejection seats?"

"Check."

Item by item they went down the list. When they finished, Tom turned his head to look at Sandra.

"Ready to launch?" he asked.

"Looks good," she said. "The minisub is functioning at one hundred percent efficiency."

"Then it's time to go."

Tom hit the release switch. The panel over the sub's berth slid shut with a loud clang. Salt water gurgled into the compartment containing the minisub. As soon as the space was completely flooded, Tom hit the launch button.

The water swirled for a moment, and then they were out, twenty feet below the platform and sinking rapidly. Tom took a mark from the gyrocompass and pointed the nose of the minisub downward. He was heading for the sunken ship where he and Rick had seen the Black Dragon's divers earlier that day.

Down and down the minisub spiraled under Tom's command. The rolling wave action that they experienced near the surface soon faded away, to be replaced by the calm water of the depths. At last the minisub halted a few feet above the ocean's floor.

"Now what?" Sandra asked. "If we show a light, anyone who's already down here will be able to see us a long time before we see them. Same thing for going active on sonar. They'll know we're here."

"We've still got a few tricks they won't be expecting," Tom said. "I'm going to try the light amplification system. Watch the screen ahead of you."

Tom looked at his own half of the sub's control panel. "Low-light TV coming on," he announced as the screen in front of him filled up with rough gray and black patches.

He gave an involuntary shiver. Here, nearly a thousand feet down at the bottom of the ocean, the currents flowed down from far northern Atlantic glaciers without ever meeting the upper air. The water outside was cold—below freezing, in fact—but the pressure of the depths kept it liquid. The interior of the minisub was damp from condensation. Even with a thick hull between the cabin and the water outside, the humid air had soon cooled to a clammy forty degrees.

"My screen looks good, Tom," Sandra said. "I have what look like shapes of rocks. Don't have your sunken ship yet, though."

"Hang on," Tom said. "I see a glow to our right. Do you have it?"

"I see it, too. Want to check it out?"

"Why not?" Tom said. "Coming right."

He put on right rudder to bring the brighter area directly in front of them. "Going ahead now."

Tom accelerated slowly until the minisub was cruising at five knots. The glow up ahead was unmistakable on his low-light monitor.

"There," he said. "Over that sea mound."

Soon Tom could see the green glow with his bare eyes. "Coming up on the lighted area," he announced. "If this isn't the Black Dragon at work, I'll eat my dive card."

He brought the minisub up and forward.

"Sandra," he said after a few seconds, "do you see what I see?"

"Yes. But I don't believe it."

Tom had trouble believing it himself. Floodlights on posts covered the expanse of ocean floor ahead of them. In the distance, Tom thought he could make out a couple of swimmers. But between the lights and the swimmers lay a sight that took his breath away: a whole graveyard of lost ships, dozens of vessels lying in long rows in the briny dark— and every single one of them had a series of gigantic holes melted through its hull.

9

Wow," SANDRA SAID IN A HUSHED VOICE. "Do you think that this is where all those ships that recently vanished in the Bermuda Triangle went to?"

"I'll give you three guesses," Tom said, "and the first two don't count. But what does the Black Dragon want with this many ships?"

"Beats me, too," Sandra replied.

"Those hulls are all made of steel," Tom mused. "That means they're not very old. And not much sediment has settled on them. I don't think they've been here long—probably less than a year. And from their configuration, they were all cargo ships."

"Got it," said Sandra. "That means those oil drums you and Rick found—"

"—must have been some ship's cargo," finished Tom.

"Do you think those divers did it?"

"I don't know for sure," Tom said, "but I think it's a pretty safe guess."

"Then I also think it's time we got out of here," Sandra told him. "If this place belongs to the Black Dragon, it's a professional operation. I'm sure they've posted some kind of guard."

"Just let me get a bit closer, so the sub's cameras and videotape systems can get positive IDs on at least some of these ships. As soon as that's finished, we're gone."

Moving low and slow, Tom inched the minisub down into the graveyard of lost ships. Silently, cameras working, the minisub eased in among the hulks.

"Look over there," Sandra said as they slid past the steel flank of one ship and drew close to the next. "See that sternboard?"

"That's the *Chevalier*, all right," said Tom, remembering the missing ship Captain O'Brien had spoken of only the previous morning. "Out of Glasgow, in Scotland. All vessels in this area are supposed to be on the lookout for her. Let's make sure to get pictures of that one."

"Uh-oh," Sandra cut in. "Something's coming this way."

Tom brought the minisub down until it hugged the ocean floor like some kind of bottom-dwelling steel fish. Keeping low, he pulled the sub deep into the shadow of the *Chevalier*'s hull and cut the water jets. Slowly the sub settled onto the bottom in a cloud of dirt and sediment.

Tom pressed his face to the viewscope. Fifty yards away, beyond the *Chevalier,* the first of the contacts appeared: two divers riding on something that looked like an underwater cargo sled. The long, open platform had steering fins and a floodlight mounted in front and a large motor and a propeller behind. The cargo area itself contained only a half-dozen black, pie-plate-shaped objects, each one about six feet across.

Good thing our cameras are still rolling, Tom thought as another sled appeared. The second sled was followed by three more.

He was just about to pull the minisub out from behind the *Chevalier* and follow the sleds when something else appeared on his monitor screen.

Tom's eyes widened in surprise. The fishermen of Saint David's Island had been right after all. From its huge fins and tail to its glowing green eyes, the new arrival was a hundred-foot-long sea monster straight out of a sailor's worst nightmare.

He shook his head to clear it. "Come on," he muttered to himself. "There's no such thing as a sea monster."

"Right you are," his sister agreed, a bit shakily. "So what *do* you think we have here?"

"I don't know, but we can find out," Tom

said. "For starters, let's see if it sounds like a sea monster."

He switched on the hydrophones and sent the output directly to the speakers in the minisub's cabin. A sound came from the speakers, a rhythmic squeaking mixed with a sound like rain falling on the surface of a pond.

"Whatever that thing is, it isn't a sea monster," Tom said after listening for a moment. "Not unless sea monsters in the Bermuda Triangle are driven by propellers."

"Okay, so it's mechanical," Sandra said. "But a mechanical what? And why is it here?"

"Give me a moment so I can switch over to infrared," Tom answered. "Then we'll find out what that thing really looks like."

He flipped another switch, and an infrared image of the sea monster filled the monitor. This time the eyes and fins and other fishlike details were missing, while a considerably more familiar shape remained.

"Hah!" Tom said at once. "Just as I thought. That's nothing but a normal, everyday submarine all tricked out with a holographic disguise. A pretty smooth one, I'll admit, to work underwater, but still—"

"If the Black Dragon is behind all this," said Sandra, "then I'm not a bit surprised that our sea creature turned out to be a submarine in a monster suit. Xavier Mace has always been really big on using holograms to hide what things look like."

"But we still don't know what he's doing down here," Tom said. He started the sub's water jets and pulled out to follow the "sea monster" and its vanguard of sleds.

"You aren't thinking about going after them, are you?" Sandra asked a bit nervously. "We've got plenty of proof in the cameras already."

"I know, but this may be a good, fast way to find out exactly what the Black Dragon is up to."

"That's what I was afraid of," Sandra told him. She sighed. "Well, Tom, never let it be said that being your sister isn't an interesting job. Follow that sea monster."

Tom let the disguised submarine pull a few hundred yards ahead, then fell in behind to cruise directly in its wake. "We're heading up again," he said after a while. "Whatever's happening is going to happen soon."

"I think I have an idea of why the sub is disguised like that," Sandra said. "Suppose Mace is doing something on the surface, something that he doesn't want to be observed doing. Why not start stories about sea monsters to frighten off the fishermen?"

"I started wondering about that in the restaurant, as soon as I heard the story," Tom agreed. "But we'll find out soon enough. We're getting close to the surface now.'"

"And another contact is starting to show up on the hydrophones," Sandra said. "Can you hear it?"

"That thump-thump-thump? Yeah. Steamship—and coming this way, too."

Tom set up a telephoto view on his monitor screen from the minisub's external cameras. "I make it a merchant ship from the hull shape," he said after a moment. "And it looks like the sea monster is on an intercept course. Let's hang back a bit and film the action for posterity."

From below, Tom and Sandra had an unobstructed view of what happened next. First the divers moved toward the surface, lugging equipment from the backs of their sleds. Then the disguised submarine came to the surface directly ahead of the merchant ship, which promptly reversed its screws, slowed, and stopped.

Meanwhile the divers swam up underneath the merchant ship and set to work slapping the large black pie plates against its hull. The disks stuck as if they were glued, although Tom suspected that powerful magnets were a more likely explanation. Once the disks were in place, the divers moved off to a safe distance. Soon a bright light flashed from first one, then another of the disks.

Jets of fire and steam burst from each disk, cutting through the merchant ship's hull in its most vulnerable spots. Wounded like that, the ship would soon be heading for the ocean bottom, where Xavier Mace's undersea graveyard waited.

And Tom had it all on film.

"Piracy on the high seas," he said. "The Black Dragon is committing out-and-out, large-scale, high-tech piracy. And we've caught him in the act."

The cargo ship's stern was now completely underwater, and its bow was sinking fast.

"Time to get out of here," Sandra said. "I think we have enough evidence to bring the international authorities in. Remember what the old-time pirates used to say about dead men telling no tales."

Tom nodded. "We've seen enough. Let's go home."

Carefully he reversed the direction of the minisub's water jets and began to back away. Then, suddenly, he saw one of the Black Dragon's divers jerk around and point directly at them.

"Uh-oh," he muttered. "We've been spotted."

The minisub was faster than any diver and probably faster than the Black Dragon's fake sea monster as well. If he and Sandra could just get out of sight, they could probably lose the pursuit and make it back to the floating platform with the proof they'd come looking for.

Tom pressed down on the right rudder as hard as he could. The minisub wheeled around toward Bermuda and the platform. He opened the engines as far as they would go, pushing for every bit of speed the minisub possessed.

With any luck, Tom decided as they sped away, the divers would dismiss the brief glimpse of the minisub as a whale sighting or as some other normal undersea encounter. But if the divers weren't the trusting sort— and being Xavier Mace's people, they probably weren't—he'd just have to get as much distance on them as he could, then try to lose them and hide until the search was over.

After that, he concluded, he could call in the United States Navy and let them handle the problem. Then, with the Black Dragon's piracy operation cleared out of the way, the Swift Enterprises experimental floating platform could resume its scientific mission off Bermuda in peace and quiet.

Suddenly his computer started beeping frantically. "Watch out, Tom!" Sandra cried.

Tom looked down at the computer screen on the control panel.

A message was blinking in red letters:

COLLISION ALERT!
COLLISION ALERT!
COLLISION ALERT!

10

Collision? Where?" Tom gasped, staring through the viewscope. The water ahead was clear. Then the hydrophone started buzzing like an electric shaver, and he understood.

"Torpedo!" he exclaimed.

He pushed the nose of the minisub down and put on maximum speed. Then he jerked back to the viewscope and searched the water ahead. He still didn't see anything. He swiveled the outside cameras to look back.

This time he saw it—a small white cylinder heading straight for them and closing rapidly. A "smart" torpedo, he realized, homing in on the noise made by the sub. The Black Dragon wouldn't settle for anything less. That meant taking evasive action wasn't going to do them any good.

Already, only seconds remained before impact. "Sandra," he called out, "grab the videotapes and put on your helmet! We have to eject!"

He tilted the minisub's nose down to the ocean floor and pulled his own helmet over his head. The plastic globe snapped into place on the dive suit's neck.

"Stand by to eject," he told Sandra. "If we're separated, get back to the platform the best way you can."

He flipped open the control console's emergency panel and jabbed the Eject button. The bottom fell out of the minisub, and compressed air blew him free. The seat fell away, and he was hurtling downward through the water.

Up above and behind him, a bright light flashed.

A heartbeat later, the shock wave from the minisub's explosion slammed into his back like a giant's hand. The blow sent Tom spinning head over heels. Jagged scraps of metal and shards of plastic streaked past him on all sides as he tumbled.

Then he was out from the debris—dizzy and disoriented from the impact of the shock wave, but alive. As soon as he was clear, he activated his jetpack and headed farther away from the wreckage of the sub.

"Sandra!" he called over the aqualingua in his helmet. "Sandra! Are you okay?"

There was no answer. A quick glance back didn't show anything or anyone following him through the murk. He hadn't seen his sister since just before the torpedo hit.

Tom glanced at the sinking wreckage of his minisub, now drifting below him. He turned up the infrared gain in his heads-up display, but even that didn't give him much help. There were heat sources down there, lots of them, but in the tangle of debris, he couldn't make out if one of them was his sister.

"Sandra!" he called out over the aqualingua. "Sandra, if you can hear me, hang on!"

Tom jetted after the pieces of the minisub as they sank. Already the baroplast of his dive suit was starting to stiffen. If he continued to head deeper, the suit would go completely rigid before long, and he knew from the earlier dive just how awkward even the simplest maneuvers would then become.

He caught up with the wreckage and began to swim through it, working as fast as he could. Among the remains of the interior, his seat was gone. He couldn't tell, though, whether the largest clump of twisted metal was Sandra's chair or whether it was part of the minisub's engines. He swam farther down beneath the wreckage, looking for the bottom hatch. It, too, was missing.

So Sandra had at least managed to eject. But if so, where was she? The aqualingua was still silent.

Time to head for the surface and check up there, Tom thought. She's probably already sitting in her life raft and waiting for me to show up.

He swam clear of the wreckage and directly into the intense white glare of artificial light. The Black Dragon's divers had found him.

A spear from a spear gun flashed past his helmet. Tom gave a flip and jetted away.

Above him was an entire web of moving lights—the Black Dragon's divers, circling the whole area of the wreck, searching for him. He changed direction again, heading still lower, his suit stiffening into a rigid shell around him as he went.

The other divers followed. From time to time their lights caught him, and he would use the jetpack to maneuver out of sight. At last he came to the ocean floor. For thousands of years the underwater currents had carved the rocks there into strange shapes—twisted spires and grotesque, misshapen columns made an undersea sculpture gallery full of holes and hiding places.

Tom found a hollowed-out little cave under an overhang and settled down to wait. By craning his neck inside the dive suit's globelike helmet, he could just glimpse the numbers on his chronolaser: three o'clock in the morning. The lateness of the hour surprised him. He supposed that the adrenaline in his system was keeping him alert.

I hope it keeps on working, he thought. This is no place to nod off and fall asleep.

To stay awake, he forced himself to do some mental calculations. Allow about an hour for the pirates to finish poking around for his body in the wreckage of the minisub. Allow another hour to sneak back up to the surface and get to the platform. That would be cutting things close on his two-hour supply of air, but Tom was sure he could make it.

Two more hours underwater would bring him up to five o'clock in the morning, still nearly an hour before first light. If Sandra had got the incriminating videotapes back to the platform, taking them to Lieutenant Commander Pena at the naval air station would take, at most, another two or three hours. And by about eight o'clock in the morning the Black Dragon's Bermuda operation would be shut down.

Movement caught Tom's eye. He saw beams of light moving through the darkness before he saw the divers. Three of them, in black diving suits, were swimming along and playing their beams of light across the ocean floor.

The divers swam by his hiding place, passing less than twenty feet away. They swam back and forth over the bits of wreckage that had landed among the rocks, then gathered together as if conferring with one another.

By the combined illumination of their lights, Tom could see the action of their dive suits in detail for the first time. The external skeleton clearly functioned to pick up the divers' muscle movements and amplify them with mechanical strength. No mater how rigid the suits became, the divers would still be able to move.

The divers moved away from the wreckage. Another thought came to Tom: Suppose the Black Dragon already had Sandra? He'd been assuming she'd made it safely to the surface, but her silence over the aqualingua could mean something else altogether.

I've got almost sixty minutes before I need to start back to the surface, he thought. If Sandra's in trouble, I shouldn't be wasting my time lurking in the dark.

Tom jetted out of his hiding place and headed after the divers, staying back just far enough to see the glow of their suit lights. He followed them past the graveyard of ships, complete with its latest addition, a cargo ship whose sternboard read *Blithe Spirit*.

Trails of tiny bubbles still streamed toward the surface from the *Spirit*'s hull. Another group of black-suited divers worked busily around her, transferring the merchant ship's cargo to one of the big undersea sleds.

Tom gave the *Spirit* a wide berth and continued after the three divers he had been following.

The water started to grow lighter. Tom saw that the source of the illumination lay somewhere beyond a ridge on the far side of the undersea graveyard. The divers swam over the ridge and disappeared from view. Tom followed. When he came to the ridge, he inched forward to peer over the crest.

Spread out below him on the ocean floor was the divers' home base.

Tom gazed down in wonder at what looked like a miniature city, a sprawling complex of crystal domes and enclosed walkways. Huge clusters of lights shone down on everything, turning the deep sea night into eternal day. Outside the structures a host of submersible craft—from the big cargo carriers to small one-man sleds—moved in and out among the domes and towers.

The three divers headed straight for one of the smaller domes. Tom remained on the ridge for a moment, studying the whole layout from that vantage point. If Sandra had been captured, the undersea complex was almost certainly where the divers would have taken her.

Tom decided that the risk involved in going farther would be worth it, if by doing so he could find his sister and help her escape from the Black Dragon's clutches. He began to jet slowly toward the undersea base.

He reached the dome through which the three divers had entered the complex and found the gateway: a small, closed door. Opening the door with his suit frozen by the pressure looked difficult but not impossible. A handle on the center had a pull ring on it.

Tom hooked the ring with his foot, then jetted away. The door swung open.

Tom jetted through. Inside, a plate against the far wall looked inviting. He pressed it with his head. The outer door swung closed, the inner door opened, and Tom jetted into the next compartment. This time, as soon as Tom had entered, the door behind him cycled shut, and the water started to drain away. As it did, the pressure eased. Tom felt the baroplast of his dive suit become flexible around him.

With the water gone, Tom pulled his feet under him and stood up. It felt good to move his arms and legs freely again. Even the extra burden of the air tanks and the lead weights on his dive belt didn't bother him. A door stood in the far wall of the air lock, a pressure door with a wheel in the center. Tom walked over and turned the wheel. With a soft whoosh of air, the door cycled open.

Tom stepped out of the air lock and found himself standing in a tiled anteroom. Immediately to his right lay a smaller room filled with wet suits and air tanks. A half dozen or so of the mechanical exoskeletons hung in a rack against the far bulkhead. A long, narrow corridor stretched out ahead of him, lit by fluorescent bulbs in recessed ceiling fixtures.

Tom took off his helmet and swim fins. There was no sense in wasting the air in his tanks if he was going to explore, and the flip-flop of the fins against the deck would give him away to any listeners. He hung the fins from a hook on his dive belt. With his helmet resting in the crook of his arm, he walked silently down the hall.

The corridor dead-ended in what looked like an elevator. The panel beside the sliding doors had a single unlabeled button. Tom hesitated for a moment, thinking that he could still turn around and go back. But if he did that, he reminded himself, he'd never find out if Sandra was a prisoner in the Black Dragon's underwater kingdom.

He pushed the button. The elevator doors slid apart, and Tom stepped in. The doors closed again, and the elevator purred into motion, carrying him not up but down, deep into the undersea recesses below the domes.

Far above, rain lashed at the wind-whipped sea. A tiny emergency life raft tossed back and forth on the waves. The sun had not yet risen; the night was black. Sandra Swift was alone, but she'd made it to the surface clutching in her hand the waterproof case containing the videotapes from the destroyed minisub.

She'd been lucky, she knew. Without her suit light on to betray her presence, she'd been thrown clear of the sub before the Black Dragon's divers could spot her. She only hoped Tom had been equally fortunate.

She groped for the raft's emergency radio and lifted it to her lips. "Tango Sierra, this is Sandra, over."

Relief washed over her as the emergency radio crackled in response. "Sandra, this is Tango Sierra. Interrogative, where are you, over."

"This is Sandra. I don't know. I'm starting my emergency homing beacon at this time."

"This is Tango Sierra, roger, we have the beacon. Hang on, we're coming to get you, over."

"This is Sandra, roger, out."

She put down the radio and sat in the life raft, looking out through the dark and rain. Maybe, she thought, her brother had deployed the life raft from his dive belt before she did and had already been rescued. Or maybe he was even now sitting in another life raft, somewhere else out here in the ocean. She didn't like to think about the third possibility at all.

Time passed. Soon a roaring of motors became audible over the sound of the wind and rain, and a beam of light shone out across the waves. She recognized the floating habitat in its hovercraft configuration.

The habitat drew up alongside the emergency raft, and Rick Cantwell popped his head out of the top hatch.

"Climb on in," he said. "We brought the fastest thing we had."

He threw her a line, and she clambered aboard. Inside, Mandy Coster was waiting.

"Where's Tom?" Mandy asked.

Sandra's heart sank. "He's not on board already?"

"No," said Mandy, her face ashen. "We were hoping he was with you."

"Well, he isn't."

The two girls looked at each other.

"Without the minisub," Mandy whispered, "this is the only craft we have that can submerge and search for Tom underwater."

Sandra clenched her fists and slowly opened them again. Then she drew a deep breath and flicked open the locker that held the dive suits. Two suits hung there.

"Seal the hatch, Rick," she said. "If Tom is still missing, we're going to keep searching until we find him."

11

TOM TENSED AS THE ELEVATOR DOOR SLID open to reveal another hallway. The elevator had traveled downward for a long time; he had to be far under the dome. Voices came from somewhere nearby.

Cold sweat covered Tom's body inside the dive suit. If his sister was in the complex at all, she couldn't yet have been taken far from the entrance, but the places where he was most likely to find her would also be the busiest. He forced himself to take a deep breath and let it out slowly. Then he peered carefully around the edge of the elevator door.

In a lounge area to his right, four men were playing cards at a table next to a soft-drink machine. The men wore uniforms of a sort: black shorts, black loafers, and black shirts with the dragon emblem printed on the front.

Tom heard the shuffle of cards. Quickly,

while the cardplayers were engrossed in picking up their new hands, he slipped out of the elevator and eased away from the right, hugging the wall as he went.

The first door he came to opened into a storeroom for office supplies. Tom eased the door closed and moved on. The second room was a dormitory, where a couple of men lay snoring in narrow bunks. The third door was locked, as was the fourth. The fifth opened into an unoccupied office containing a desk with a computer on top of it.

"Bingo," Tom whispered. If he could tap into the Black Dragon's computer, perhaps he could find Sandra and learn something about Mace's plans as well. He stepped in and closed the door behind him.

The computer was already on. Tom brought up the main menu, then called up a word-processing program. In the directory, he found a series of reports concerning the divers' progress in building the undersea base. He started skimming through them as fast as he could.

Tom had gotten only to the third report—dated over a year before—when a quiet voice spoke behind him.

"Please don't move, Tom Swift. Keep your hands where I can see them."

Tom swallowed. Then he raised his hands to surrender.

"You have the right attitude," the speaker

said. "Now stand up and turn around, very slowly."

Tom did as he was told and saw that his captor was a woman in her midtwenties, a redhead in a yellow one-piece bathing suit. She was holding an electric stun gun.

"Walk through that doorway over there," she ordered. "Mr. Mace wants to talk with you."

Tom looked at the stun gun. "Yes, ma'am," he said.

A man was waiting behind a desk in the next room, with another man—a bodyguard, Tom guessed—standing at his side. The seated man was in his late forties or early fifties, neatly dressed in a blue suit with a white turtleneck shirt. His dark hair was shot with gray.

"Good morning, Tom," the seated man said. "Would you care for a seat?"

The woman with the stun gun pulled a chair away from the wall and set it in front of the desk. She waved the gun at the chair and favored Tom with a meaningful smile.

Tom sat down.

"What, you don't have anything to say?" the older man said. "Ah, but I haven't yet introduced myself. I looked much different the last time we met. I am Xavier Mace. The gentleman beside me is Anton, and the dear lady who stands behind you is Felicity. Now, what do you say?"

"Don't I even get to make a phone call?" Tom asked.

"The young these days, they have no respect," Mace said, his eyes crinkling with good humor. "Really, Tom, I am quite fond of you. Did you know that at one time I dated the girl who would later be your mother? If she hadn't met your father, the estimable Mr. Swift—why, you might have been my own son. In some ways I feel that you ought to have been."

Tom managed to control his disgust. "For someone who's fond of me," he said finally, "you have a strange way of showing it. In fact, I've lost count of the number of times you've tried to kill me."

"Tried to kill you? You mistake me." The man who called himself Mace shook his head sadly. "If I had wanted to kill you, Tom, you most assuredly would be dead."

The nightmare unreality of the conversation combined with a sleepless night was already starting to make Tom's head whirl, but he pressed on. "Assuming just for the sake of argument that you really aren't trying to kill me," he said, "would you mind telling me what you *are* doing?"

He could have sworn that the older man's eyes twinkled. "Tom," said Mace, "I'm glad you asked that. Really, I am. I want to share this with you."

The Black Dragon nodded to Anton. The

man walked to the side of the room and turned a switch. The room lights dimmed, and lasers blinked to life in the ceiling fixtures. Where the beams met, a holographic image appeared.

"The floor of the northern Atlantic," Mace said, "modeled in three dimensions. You can see the mid-Atlantic ridge over there—Europe to the east, North America to the west—I'm sure you recognize all the major features."

"Most of them," said Tom. "But I've seen more impressive holography from you than this stuff. The disguise you're wearing right now, for example. Or that do-it-yourself sea-monster kit."

"You have no faith, Tom. That's your main problem," Mace said. "Look at the area around Bermuda. Felicity, show him what I'm talking about."

The redheaded woman touched a spot on the wall. The holographic view of the under-sea area around Bermuda enlarged and expanded until it took up most of the room. On this scale, Tom could even make out the domes and towers of the Black Dragon's base.

"Did you know that Bermuda lies on a tectonic plate of its own?" Mace asked. "And do you see where this undersea city of mine is located? Watch."

The seabed began to twist and writhe, and the part of the bottom where the city lay began to move upward. Before long, the domed complex in the holographic scale model occupied an island rising above the Atlantic waves.

"Behold," said Mace. "The new Atlantis—my fair city beneath the sea, rising newborn from the ocean foam."

"Okay, so it works fine in the lab," said Tom. "But how are you going to make it happen out in the field?"

The Black Dragon smiled. "I have located the weakest point in the Bermuda Plate. If a bomb of the proper size is placed in it, the plate will be destabilized enough to raise an entirely new island from the ocean floor."

"You realize," Tom said carefully, "that any tectonic movements big enough to lift up a new land mass would have bad side effects. The shoreline as far away as the United States would be hit by giant earthquakes and tidal waves."

Mace shrugged. "So? To make an omelet, one must break eggs. There's no guesswork involved. I know exactly what will happen. Show him, Felicity."

The simulation shrank until it once again showed the whole north Atlantic.

"Begin," the Black Dragon said.

The simulation shimmered briefly, and Tom saw the scale model of the islands begin to shake.

"That," said Mace, "is a quake of approximately nine point eight on the Richter scale. The epicenter is not far from this very room. Now the tectonic plates have begun to move."

The islands continued to quiver. The ocean pulled away from the shore in a rush, leaving the continental shelf almost dry. Out in the middle of the Atlantic, the waters began to pile up into a huge wave. Slowly at first, then faster and faster, the wave began to move back toward the Caribbean. As Tom watched, the tidal wave swept over Bermuda and the other islands, completely covering them.

"Fortunately," Mace observed as the wave continued toward the coasts of Florida and Central America, "I've already sold all of my oceanfront properties for a tidy profit. Once the waters recede, I can buy them back at my leisure for considerably less."

Tom swallowed hard. "But the *people*—"

"What are the people to me?" the Black Dragon asked. "I don't know any of them personally."

He gestured at Felicity. She touched another spot on the wall, and the room lights came back up. Mace stood and walked around from behind his desk. Anton and Felicity moved into position on either side of Tom.

"Come along," Mace said. "But please, no tricks, or Anton and Felicity will have to hurt you."

Together they walked to the elevator and

rode it up to the entry level. The Black Dragon led the way to the end of the long corridor.

"Stay here a moment," Mace said. He went into the room with the equipment and emerged a few minutes later dressed in the same kind of diving suit his workers wore, except that his suit was all white with a large black dragon on the chest. He turned away briefly to put a globular helmet on his head.

When Mace turned back, Tom saw that the globe was silvered on the inside. Even outside in the water, if the holographic disguise should fail, no one would see the Black Dragon's true features. Then, with Anton's help, Mace put one of the powered exoskeletons over his suit.

"Come now," Mace said to Tom. "We're going to take a trip outside. We don't communicate with anything as crude as that aqualingua of yours—a device, by the way, with limited range and power, not at all up to your usual standard. My spies at Swift Enterprises didn't consider it worth stealing, I'm afraid. But we can still talk. Felicity?"

The redhead opened her hand to show Tom a small device that looked like a button earring decorated with a tiny computer chip. She stepped forward and clipped it to Tom's earlobe. Tom shivered as the metal pinched his skin.

"I'd be a poor host if I didn't show you my

entire operation," Mace said. "So I'll accompany you outside for a little while."

The archcriminal nodded at Anton. The bodyguard took Tom's diving helmet and snapped it into place on Tom's head. Oxygen began to hiss into Tom's suit.

"Can you hear me?" Mace asked. The device clipped to Tom's earlobe carried Mace's voice right into Tom's helmet.

"Yes," Tom said. "I hear you. But where are we going, and why do we need to talk?"

"All in good time, Tom Swift," said Mace as four more divers in black suits came out of the equipment room. Anton opened the air lock, and Mace stepped into the compartment. The divers hustled Tom in after him.

The door swung closed, and the compartment began to fill with water. Tom felt his suit begin to stiffen and then freeze entirely.

"Ah, yes, the disadvantages of crude baroplast," Mace said. "You notice how I solved that problem? As you will see very shortly, I have managed to solve all my problems."

The outer door opened, and the Dragon's divers hauled Tom through it. Outside, the lights were still burning brightly over the field of ships.

"Come with me," Xavier Mace said, and he led the way through the sunken hulks to the top of the small sea mountain overlooking the base. He floated there, waiting while his men pulled Tom into place beside him.

The Black Dragon glanced at Tom. "Ah, the gauges on your tanks show there's not much air remaining. Well, it doesn't matter. You won't be needing it—you aren't going far."

Xavier Mace turned to gaze out over his underwater city. "Look at it, Tom," he said. "My fair city lying alone far down beneath the unsuspecting surface world. Isn't it beautiful? After it rises above the ocean, I shall rule the world."

"Right," Tom said without enthusiasm. "But tell me one thing. If you're going to rule the whole world, why are you sinking those ships?"

"To get supplies for my new country, Tom." The Black Dragon's voice sparkled with enthusiasm. "Every time I set up headquarters in one country or another, the government gets upset with me and makes me move. What I need, of course, is my own country, where I *am* the government. At present, however, every bit of real estate on earth is claimed by an already-existing country. So I am going to create a land that has never in history belonged to anyone at all—a piece of ground lifted from the ocean bottom. And because of the fondness I've always had for you, Tom, I'm going to offer you a half share in all my enterprises if you agree to work with me.

Think of it, Tom Swift—you could help me rule the world!''

Tom looked for a moment at the silvered globe of the Black Dragon's helmet. He wished he could see the face inside, so he could try to fathom what Mace truly meant by his extraordinary offer. But speculation was useless, he knew. Even if he tried to buy time by pretending to accept the offer, Mace wasn't going to give him a chance to get away before the earthquake started.

"No," he said, and tried to jet away upward, out of the reaches of the Black Dragon and his four divers. But other divers were waiting in the water above. They caught Tom easily and brought him back.

"I was afraid you'd react like that," the Black Dragon said. "A pity, really. But no matter. The time has come," he said, "to complete my plan. I've acquired a particularly powerful explosive to begin the process— eighty pounds of nitrolium."

That was like the Black Dragon, Tom reflected. Nitrolium had originally been developed by Swift Enterprises for demolition work. Even a few pounds of it could blow up a building. Eighty pounds of nitrolium would generate the world's largest nonnuclear explosion.

Mace gestured to the divers. They wrapped a length of chain around Tom's upper arms and body and then around his wrists. To the end of the chain one diver shackled a heavy black box with a digital readout on the front.

"What a pity," the Black Dragon said, "that you designed your diving suit so badly. How frustrated you will be, knowing that the bomb is dangling from your wrists—and you can't do anything to take it off!"

12

THE BLACK DRAGON'S DIVERS HAULED TOM over to one of the big undersea sleds. They deposited him on the cargo platform, helpless in his pressure-stiffened dive suit, and chained another large block of metal to his feet.

"Five hundred pounds of lead weights are now chained to your ankles," Tom heard the Black Dragon say over the earphone, "to make certain that you sink quickly enough. It's very important that you reach the proper depth before the explosion takes place or the island-building process might not work."

"You're insane," Tom gasped.

"Maybe," the Black Dragon said, his tone of voice indicating that he was seriously considering the possibility. "But it really doesn't matter to you anymore."

The sled got under way, cruising silently along the ocean floor. The Black Dragon and his divers swam alongside. They soon came to an area crisscrossed with massive cracks in the ocean floor. There, dark plumes of super-heated water rose out of underground springs. Around the fissures in the seabed flourished a huge colony of giant tube worms—ten-foot-long creatures that drew their nourishment from the hot, sulfur-laden water. Their blood-red bodies swayed snakelike in the underwater currents.

Mace pointed at one of the fissures. "You see that crevice there, Tom? That's the one you'll be going into. If you have any last words, you ought to say them now."

The sled was positioned over the crevice. The four divers towed Tom and his weights into position above the dark crack in the seabed. Mace swam over and set the timer on the bomb.

"Goodbye, Tom," Mace said.

The divers released their grip. Weighted down by lead and nitrolium, Tom began sinking toward the fissure.

"An interesting problem to occupy your mind in its last minutes, don't you think?" Mace's voice sounded in Tom's ear. "The water is already getting hotter around you. At the same time, of course, the water pressure is also increasing. At some point, the pressure will be even more than what Swift Enterprises baroplast can handle, but by then you may already have perished from the heat.

115

And of course, if neither the pressure nor the heat kills you, the nitrolium explosion certainly will. The question is, which one is it going to be?"

The Black Dragon's mocking laughter faded as Tom continued to sink into the fissure.

Tom lowered his chin and activated his jetpack. His descent slowed but didn't stop. With all the extra weight he was carrying, the jetpack didn't have the power to pull him out. If he wanted to get free, somehow he would have to rid himself of his burden of metal and explosives.

According to the digital readout projected on Tom's helmet, he had another twenty minutes' worth of air. The lithium batteries would run his jetpack at full power for half that time. And the nitrolium probably wouldn't explode for at least half an hour—the Black Dragon still had to evacuate his underwater base in preparation for the explosion. That would give Tom a little while in which to act.

Tom moved his fingers inside his rigid gloves. He wished he'd had time to test the chronolaser a bit more, to see if it really would pick up the tiny changes in capacitance in his wrist even through a pressure-hard baroplast suit. Then, just as he was about to give up hope altogether, there it was—the bright beam of light from his laser, shooting out into the sea in front of him.

By the beam's glow, he could see rough

rock walls sliding by him as he continued downward. He flexed his fingers again in a different sequence. The laser's beam grew brighter as it increased in power. He forced himself not to panic but to continue steadily and methodically through the settings.

Level two . . . level three . . . level four.

On four, the laser beam reached its highest intensity. If he made a mistake and cut through his suit, he'd be dead within seconds. But the lead weights were chained to his body. That meant they were dangling far below him.

Tom activated the jetpack again, this time forcing himself downward. Maneuvering in the narrow fissure by the action of his water jets alone was trickier work than Tom had ever done, but at last the chain fastening the weight to his ankles came into position in front of the laser beam. After that, it took him five tries to bring the chain close enough for him to slice into it. Finally, he connected, and the lead weights fell away.

With his jetpack on high, Tom shot upward like a bullet from a gun. The bomb was still chained to his wrists, where he couldn't bring the laser to bear. But then, in sudden despair, he realized that it didn't matter.

He'd been too cautious in freeing himself from the lead weights, and now he was running out of time. The readout in his helmet told him that he would have no air to breathe or power for his jetpack while he was still hundreds of feet from the surface.

Sandra Swift keyed the radio in the sea habitat. With Rick and Mandy, she'd been searching the waters where the sub had gone down for over an hour, with no luck.

"Tango Sierra," she said into the radio, "this is Tango Sierra Two. Interrogative, any word from Tom, over."

"This is Tango Sierra," the answer came back. "Reference your last, negative, over."

"Roger, out," Sandra said, and replaced the handset. "Looks like it's still up to us."

"Tom's probably out of air by now, you know," Rick said glumly.

Mandy was watching the sonar screen. "Rick," she said, "shut up and look over here. What do you see?"

"Looks like a small target heading up, fast," Rick said after watching the echo for two more pings. "Sandra, do you think that's Tom?"

"I don't know," Sandra said. "There were lots of divers down there. But I'm going to take a quick look, anyway. What have we got to lose?"

She switched the habitat into submersible mode and started heading it downward.

"Wait a minute," Rick said. "We're getting more echoes, farther down. Looks like more divers, and they're following the first one up!"

"It has to be Tom, then!" Mandy exclaimed. "The others are chasing him!"

Sandra told herself to avoid jumping to optimistic conclusions. "Could be."

Then the first contact faltered and slowed. Its upward progress ceased. It started drifting downward again at the speed of an object falling in water.

"I don't like the looks of this," Mandy said. "That *has* to be Tom. And if he's sinking like that, he must be in bad trouble."

"That's okay," said Sandra. "We're going to get him."

"But look at the depth!" Rick exclaimed. "That target is already at five hundred feet and heading down fast. That's below the level we can take this habitat without the windows bursting in."

"Forget the windows," Sandra said. "Put on your diving suits. I'm taking this thing down!"

Without waiting, she pushed the habitat's control lever to its full down position. Water swirled upward past the viewports, leaving streams of tiny bubbles in the beams from the habitat's exterior lights.

Rick and Mandy scrambled into the deep-diving suits from the habitat's locker. Sandra settled her own globular helmet back into place.

"Two hundred feet," Rick called out, returning to the depth gauge as soon as he'd suited up. "Two hundred fifty. Three hundred."

The plastic in the windows groaned and started to bulge inward.

"Three hundred fifty feet," called Rick. "Four hundred. The target's to the right of us, one hundred ninety feet away."

Sandra altered course. "Approaching crush depth," she called. "Everybody hang on."

"Four hundred fifty feet," Rick said. "Four hundred seventy-five."

A thin stream of water appeared at the edge of one of the windows. The water shot like a solid bar across the interior of the habitat and turned into spray as it struck against the inner wall.

"Take a mark on the target right now," ordered Sandra. "We're going to lose the electronics when the windows go."

"Straight ahead, range one hundred feet," Rick called, "and we're—"

The rest of his words were lost in the crash of all the windows giving way at once. The sonar screen before him shattered inward as turbulent water came smashing through the interior of the habitat.

Tom jetted toward the surface, the bomb chained to his wrists dragging in the water and slowing him down. Someone must have been watching the sonar screens at the Black Dragon's undersea headquarters. Far below, he could see lights moving as the Black Dragon's divers began to follow.

He looked upward. The surface still wasn't in sight. The clock readout in his helmet said 0519. A few minutes before navigational twilight, a solid hour before sunrise.

His air was close to flat, and the power supply in his jetpack was even lower. The depth in his heads-up display read 1,012 feet. He passed the thousand-foot mark and kept going up.

Tom knew he wasn't going to make it to the surface, but he would do his best to see how far he could get. Whatever happened, at least the bomb wouldn't go off in the crevice and start the earthquake. He'd made sure of that. Still, even an undersea burst of the size the Black Dragon had talked about would create a tidal wave high enough to wipe Bermuda clean.

Tom glanced below him. The lights were gaining. *They* didn't have eighty-pound weights chained to them.

He heard a sonar ping in the water. Up above him was a light, far away but coming down. Tom recognized the sea habitat.

Somebody from the platform was coming down to get him.

Then the power to the jetpack failed. The lithium batteries expended, the jets no longer propelled him toward the surface. The numbers in his depth gauge stopped, then began drifting downward as he sank.

"Go back!" Tom called over the aqualingua. "Get back! You're all going to get killed!"

But they didn't hear him—or if they heard him, they didn't listen. The habitat kept right on descending.

He saw the habitat shudder. Air bubbles burst out of it from every side. Even through his helmet he could hear the thud and whoosh as the windows crashed in. The habitat rocked before his eyes and began to descend even faster. It was sinking just as he was sinking, pulled downward by the weight of the Black Dragon's nitrolium bomb.

Tom was passing five hundred feet on the way to the bottom again, with only five minutes of air remaining, when the projections on his heads-up display failed.

"Have to fix the power supply on the read-outs when I redesign," he muttered.

Then he realized he wouldn't have the chance to redesign his invention. He was locked in a diving suit frozen as hard as iron by the pressure, with minutes to go before he smothered in his own carbon dioxide, drifting down with a time bomb that would go off at any second. And his friends, his would-be rescuers, were dead, too.

Loose papers and debris swirled in the water inside the sinking habitat. The interior lights had all gone out. The exterior ones were on a separate circuit and would continue to shine for a while longer.

Sandra Swift's diving suit had frozen around her when the pressure increased. She bent her head and with her chin keyed the aqualingua in her helmet.

"Mandy, Rick," she called. "Can you hear me? Do either of you see the target?"

"Yeah, got you," Rick's voice replied. "But it looks like we've lost contact with Tom."

Then Mandy's voice came over the aqualingua speaker. "Over here!" she called. "I see someone in a yellow suit. It looks like Tom, but he's got something tied onto him."

"Okay," Sandra said. "I'm going out."

Before anyone could protest, she activated her jetpack and sped through the broken viewport in front of her. Once in the sea, she looked around. There it was—a body in a yellow baroplast diving suit.

She turned in that direction and jetted down. Her right arm was still bent in a crook from the way she had been holding the controls when the pressure hit. She came up even with Tom, linked her arm under his, and began to pull him toward the still-sinking habitat.

Tom opened his eyes and looked at her. She saw him key his aqualingua.

". . . bomb . . ." came the faint whisper inside her helmet. ". . . go away . . . bomb."

DON'T WORRY ABOUT IT, TOM," SANDRA REASsured her brother. "I've got you now. We're going to get away."

She jetted toward the habitat, pulling Tom behind her. Far below, she saw a swarm of lights rising through the water toward her— more divers coming after Tom. The divers were still far away, but her brother's half-conscious body, weighted down by the box chained to his wrists, was slowing her progress more than she'd expected.

Then another dive-suited form came hurtling downward out of the broken window of the habitat.

"Hang on, Sandra!" Mandy Coster called out over the aqualingua. "I'll help you bring him in."

Together the two girls dragged and pushed Tom the last few feet to the viewport of the habitat. By tugging and shoving, they got him partway in, but the black box chained to his wrists was too big to fit through. He was stuck half in and half out, with the heavy box dangling on the outside.

"Rick, you try to hold on to him," Sandra said over the aqualingua. "We'll have to take him up the way he is."

Sandra jetted around to the next viewport, with Mandy following. They swam into the flooded habitat—a dark, curving tunnel illuminated only by the reflection of the exterior lights. Through the blue-gray murk, Sandra could see Rick, his dive suit frozen in the half-sitting position he'd held at the moment the pressure hit.

Somehow, though, Rick had managed to work the crook of one arm under Tom's dive belt. Now he was letting his own weight act as a counterbalance to the box hanging from Tom's wrists.

I hope he can hang on when we head for the surface, Sandra thought. Because I haven't got the time to take us up slow and easy.

"Look out!" Mandy called over the aqualingua. "The Black Dragon's divers are closing in!"

Sandra glanced outside the habitat and saw a diver swimming toward the unblocked viewport. His black suit had a mechanical exoskeleton, and Xavier Mace's dragon logo was painted in black on white on its chest. He carried a spear gun in one hand. When he reached the viewport, he raised the spear gun and took aim.

The spear missed Sandra by inches and was lost in the dark interior. The man drew a knife and began to swim through the opening.

"Going up *right now!*" Sandra shouted.

She jetted away from the viewport toward the center wall of the habitat and the slap-switch labeled Emergency Surface and butted the switch with her head. The habitat shuddered as the ballast in its bottom fell away. With a bone-drilling whine, the engines that had been forcing the habitat toward the bottom reversed their action. The vessel shot upward.

Sandra fell down onto the deck with a thump. Not far away, Mandy tumbled hard against a bulkhead as the habitat hurtled upward through the water. Over at the viewport, Rick still had a hold on Tom's dive belt.

The Black Dragon's diver was still with them, caught halfway in the viewport by the press of the water rushing by outside. Up they went, faster than a rising elevator. Sandra could feel the pressure easing, her baroplast suit getting flexible again. As soon as she could, she pushed herself off the deck. The Black Dragon's diver was starting to work his way into the habitat.

Sandra jetted feet-first at the diver, hitting him with both heels and smashing him back

126

out the window. He fell away as the habitat continued toward the surface.

They burst from the sea in a splash of foam. Water cascaded outward from the smashed-in viewports. Rain hissed on the surface of the ocean, and the habitat rocked on the waves. The lights of the floating platform shone above the waves to the east.

"Hurry," said Mandy. "Get Tom's helmet off before he runs out of air."

Together, she and Rick pulled the helmet off. Tom was unconscious but still breathing. While Mandy worked at reviving Tom, Sandra took the habitat's controls—the emergency mechanicals, not dependent on electrical power—and steered for the platform. The habitat's interior was only half-flooded now. Loose debris and equipment sloshed back and forth in the waist-high water. Rick waded over to the tool locker and located a bolt cutter.

"Let's get these chains off Tom's wrist, so we can pull him all the way inside," he said.

"Keep that box, though," said Sandra. "It might be important. You can tie off the chain to one of the seats or something."

As Rick finished cutting the chain, Tom began to stir.

"Bomb," he muttered. "Earthquake. Going to go off."

"It's okay, buddy," Rick said. "You're safe now."

"No," Tom said, struggling to a sitting position. "There's a bomb—eighty pounds of nitrolium. We have to disarm it."

"Wow," Rick breathed. "If they want a bang that big, why not just use a nuke?"

Tom stood unsteadily. "Because Xavier Mace is planning to live here after it goes off," he said. "Rick, could you get me a new power pack and air supply from the locker? I have to get that bomb."

"We're already up on the surface and heading back for the floating platform," Mandy said. "Wherever the Black Dragon planted his bomb, it's a long way down from here."

"You don't understand." Tom's voice was urgent as he put on the fresh air tanks and inserted the new power cartridges into his dive suit. "The black box I was chained to *is* the bomb."

"Don't worry, then. We still have it in tow," Rick said. "When's it supposed to go off?"

"I don't know," Tom said. "So we'd better act fast."

As soon as the habitat was tied up alongside the floating platform, Sandra and Mandy hurried away to the bridge to inform Captain O'Brien of Tom's rescue and to warn the platform crew about the Black Dragon's bomb. When Rick started to follow, Tom flung out a hand to stop him.

"Stick around for a moment, Rick," he said. "I may need a hand."

Tom dropped down into the water beside the bomb. For the first time, he was able to see the digital readout on its face. The numbers read 2:24. As Tom watched, the readout changed to 2:23.

That's how long we've got before it goes off, he thought. And the box looks as if it was sealed. There's no way to get inside and stop the countdown.

He swam back to the surface. "Rick," he called, "give me a hand. We have to get this thing out of the water. I can't disarm it. If it blows up in the water, there's going to be a tidal wave that'll turn all of Bermuda into bare rock."

With Rick pulling on the chains from above the surface and Tom pushing from below, they succeeded in lifting the bomb onto the top of the habitat. "Thanks," said Tom to Rick as they finished lashing it down. "Now untie the habitat and get out of here."

Rick hesitated a moment, then scrambled out and over to the deck of the floating platform. Tom climbed down into the habitat and started the engine again. He moved the mechanical linkage to hovercraft mode and started the habitat into motion with the rudder tied down, heading eastward out to sea—away from the floating platform and the island of Bermuda.

Tom turned to the throttle. He jammed it all the way forward for maximum speed and shoved a water-logged record book behind the lever to keep it in position. The bomb was out of the water, and he was taking it as far as possible from people. That would lessen the effect of the blast and save as many lives as possible.

The habitat picked up speed. In hovercraft mode it could move very fast indeed.

Tom looked back and saw the platform receding in the distance. He smiled. Now if only the bomb would hold off exploding until the platform was a safe distance away.

On the platform, Rick ran up to the bridge. The others were already there, along with O'Brien and Louis.

"Where's Tom?" Mandy asked.

"He's on the habitat," panted Rick. "With the bomb."

"Isn't he finished with it yet?" Sandra demanded.

Louis Armont shook his head. "Disarming a bomb can be a tricky process, even for one who has many years of training. I fear young Tom has realized that he does not have enough time."

Mandy stared out at the ocean. "You mean—"

Rick nodded. "He's trying to get it as far away from us as possible before it blows."

Through the bridge windows, they could see the habitat heading away at high speed.

"Shut off the sonar," O'Brien ordered. "If Tom's going to swim back, we don't want to break his eardrums."

The habitat vanished to the east. On the bridge of the floating platform, everybody watched and waited in tense silence. Seconds later a glow appeared against the eastern sky. Then a column of fire and smoke soared skyward—a glowing cloud, nearly two miles high, with a luminescent mushroom head a mile across. A moment later came the soundwave, a rumbling roar louder than any thunder. Over the sea, the shock wave raced like a ripple in the water, barely visible in the light from the explosion and the first hints of graying dawn in the eastern sky.

"Look forward!" called Katie Booth. "Someone coming on board."

"It's Tom!" exclaimed Mandy.

Moments later, Tom appeared on the bridge, still wearing his baroplast dive suit and carrying the plastic fishbowl helmet. "Okay," he said when he arrived on the bridge, "that's one thing down. But we have to get away from here. The Black Dragon doesn't dare let us get back with the news of what he's been doing."

He looked at O'Brien. "I don't think the utility boat will take us out of here fast enough. We'd better ride the platform in."

"No problem," O'Brien said. "I'd already decided to cut the mission short, anyway, so my crew and I spent most of last night preparing for a high-speed run back home."

"Okay," Tom said. "Let's go."

O'Brien picked up the intercom connecting him to the engineering section. "Secure the stabilizers," he called. "Feed forward power."

The platform began to roll slightly as the stabilizers were shut off. Only the water jets at the stern remained on-line to give the platform forward motion.

"Okay, Booth," O'Brien ordered, "take the wheel. Come to course two-seven-zero. We're heading back to the United States."

The platform picked up speed, its deep V-shaped hull, which was concealed beneath its squared-off top, cutting through the water.

"Retract stabilizer vanes, stand by to deploy hydrofoils," O'Brien said. "Estimated time to landfall, Cape Hatteras light, nine hours and forty minutes."

With the foils extended, the platform rode on slim pylons above the sea, cutting through the water at nearly sixty knots. Silver spray flew away from either side of the platform's bow, and a white wake boiled behind them. Overhead the sun broke through the clouds, as the storm of the night before began to pass.

Tom and Rick stood on the bridge wing, the wind ruffling their hair. "Looks like we've escaped," Rick said to Tom.

"Escaped isn't good enough," Tom said. "For all we know, the Black Dragon has a second nitrolium bomb sinking into that rift of his right now."

Rick shook his head. "I don't think you can *get* one hundred and sixty pounds of nitrolium, no matter how hard you try. Not even if you're Xavier Mace."

"Maybe not nitrolium," said Tom. "But Mace isn't going to give up just because I got away."

"You shouldn't be such a pessimist," said Rick. "We've got the proof we need to shut down Mace's operations on the high seas, and you kept him from blowing up Bermuda. What more do you want?"

"I don't know," Tom said. "But I keep feeling that it isn't enough, that there's something more."

The water ahead of the foil-borne platform roiled and bubbled, and a gigantic, green-eyed creature rose out of the depths.

"It's the sea monster!" yelled Rick.

"Sea monster my foot!" Tom yelled back. "It's the Black Dragon and his submarine!"

O'Brien saw it, too. "Right full rudder!" he called. "Reverse thrust. Increase rudder to right hard."

The rapid ringing of the collision alarm filled the platform. O'Brien sounded five rapid blasts on the platform's whistle. "Hang on!" he shouted.

The platform slowed and swerved to the right, but it was moving too fast, and the sub had surfaced too close. The two vessels met in a shuddering crash, followed by the high, brittle sound of shattering glass and the scream of tearing metal.

The air around Tom filled with saltwater spray and sparks. The platform kicked and bucked like a wild animal as it drove over the Black Dragon's submarine at full speed.

There was a giant snapping noise. The platform lurched and started to fall into the water.

"Hold on!" Tom shouted. "We've lost the hydrofoil pylons!"

THE PLATFORM CRASHED INTO THE OCEAN, spraying water in all directions. Tom hung on tightly to the railing of the bridge wing and looked back at the platform's wake.

The Black Dragon's sea monster was in bad shape. The deep keel of the oceangoing platform had plowed directly into Mace's vessel, destroying whatever mechanism generated its holographic disguise. Nothing remained of the monster but a submarine wallowing on its side in the water.

The sub rolled ponderously upright. Tom saw a huge gash along the top of the vessel, aft near the vertical rudder. Then the sub wallowed again and began to go down by the stern. For a moment its bow stuck out of the water like a pointing finger before the Black Dragon's submarine slid beneath the waves.

"Come on, Rick," Tom said. "There are people on that sub. We have to try to save them."

"They tried to kill you."

"It doesn't matter," said Tom. "They're people, and they're in trouble. It's the law of the sea."

He snapped on his helmet and ran down to the main deck. The floating platform wasn't doing too well itself, Tom noticed. It was listing heavily to port and was down by the bow. He slipped over the side into the water. A minute later, three more dive-suited figures joined him: Rick, Mandy, and Sandra.

"I still think you're crazy," said Rick over the aqualingua. "But we aren't about to let you dive alone."

"Then let's go," said Tom.

He switched on his lights and activated his jetpack. With the new power and air supply he'd put into the suit just before abandoning the emergency habitat, he should have plenty of air left for what he needed to do. Down he went, following the trail of bubbles from the doomed submarine. At last he caught up with it.

He could see why no one had left the sub. The escape capsule was there, still on the foredeck where it had tried to launch but trapped by bent metal and wreckage from the collision. Tom jetted down and grabbed a handhold on the outside of the capsule. He banged on the side of the capsule with his other hand. From inside, he could hear a dull thumping sound as someone pounded back. The person gave three short raps, three long, and another three short—SOS.

"Someone's still alive," Tom said to his friends over the aqualingua.

"And heading for the bottom," Mandy said. "Straight into all the dark water that's boiling up from below."

"It's an underwater vent," Tom said. "That's boiling water you see coming up—like a hot spring, only much larger and much hotter. The darkness in the water is from dissolved minerals. Mace was going to drop me into something like that."

"He's going to go into one himself if we can't think of something real quick," Sandra said.

From aft on the sub came a heavy thump, as an interior bulkhead gave way and imploded under pressure.

"Hear that?" said Tom. "We don't have as much time as we thought. And my suit is stiffening already. If we don't rescue these people soon, we may never rescue them."

Activating his water jets, Tom circled the escape pod attached to the sinking submarine. This time he thought he spotted the source of the jam—a bent metal bar.

"Okay," he said, still jetting down to keep even with the sinking craft. "Looks like we've located the problem. I'll try to cut it with my chronolaser."

Tom switched on the laser to its lowest setting and placed the red dot on the bent metal bar. Level by level, he increased the setting of the beam until it had reached its highest intensity.

"Rick, Mandy, steady me," he said. "I don't want to grab a handhold and get stuck when the pressure freezes my suit completely. Sandra, you keep a lookout."

Down they went as Tom worked on the iron bar. At last the beam from the chronolaser cut through the last fraction of an inch, and the cut pieces of the bar floated away. The escape pod tumbled free of the doomed submarine but still didn't begin to head upward. Instead, it hung motionless in the water, as if something held it suspended.

"The flotation gear in the pod must be damaged," Rick said. "You did all that work for nothing."

"Maybe not," said Tom. "I still have the emergency life-raft cartridge attached to my dive belt. How about the rest of you?"

"Yes," from Rick. "Yes," from Mandy. "No," from Sandra.

"Sorry I'm the odd one out," Tom's sister added. "But I used mine when we ejected from the minisub."

"With luck, three will be enough," Tom said. "We'll attach the life rafts to the escape pod and inflate them. The extra buoyancy should carry the pod to the surface."

"The pressure has stiffened our suits too much," Rick protested. "How are we going to deploy the life rafts if we can't use our hands?"

Tom thought for a moment. "Okay," he said. "I'll go inside the sub and see if I can find one of those exoskeletons the Black Dragon's people use. If I can get into it, maybe we can save some lives."

"If you get trapped in there, you'll be dead yourself," said Rick.

"That's a risk I'll have to take," Tom replied.

He jetted down to the sinking submarine, alongside the gaping hole in its skin. "I'm going in now," he said over the aqualingua. "If I'm not back in fifteen minutes, head for the surface without me."

Carefully Tom made his way past the jagged metal edges of the gash in the sub. His aqualingua fell silent as he passed out of line of sight from his friends.

The interior of the submarine was a dark mass of wreckage. Floating bits of gear swirled in the beam of Tom's suit light. In the forward section of the sub, upward from where Tom swam, a bulkhead had collapsed.

"Let's see," Tom muttered under his breath. "If I were Xavier Mace, where would I keep my dive suits."

To his surprise, a voice answered him. "Tom? Tom Swift? This is one pleasure I did *not* expect."

"Mace!" Tom gasped. He realized that in the excitement of his escape, he'd completely forgotten the Black Dragon's clip-mounted voice transmitter. "Where are you, Mace?"

"In my cabin, of course," the familiar voice answered. "I'm afraid that the damage to this boat has totally blocked my way out. Perhaps, if I am lucky, you will also be caught, and we can perish together."

"Not if I can help it," Tom said. "Listen, Mace. You can still save the rest of your people. They're trapped in the escape pod. I can't get them to the surface unless I can find one of your powered diving frames."

"Don't waste your time playing the hero," Mace said. "Felicity and Anton and the others knew from the start that working for me would bring them fabulous wealth if they succeeded, while failure would bring them nothing but death."

"The wages you pay your people aren't my problem," Tom said, still swimming upward with the aid of his jetpack. "Will you help them, or won't you?"

There was silence for a moment. Then the Black Dragon asked, "Where are you right now?"

Tom glanced around, looking for some kind of landmark. "I'm in the engine room," he said after a moment. "Near bulkhead one-ninety-seven."

"Excellent," said Mace. "I know where you are. Go forward until you see a plate labeled Generators."

Tom swam cautiously forward. He had no reason to trust Mace, but he had no choice, either. "Okay," he said. "I'm there."

"You should see a vertical ladder," Mace said. "It leads down to the lower engineering storeroom and up to the escape hatch."

"Okay. I'm on the ladder."

"In the escape hatch, you will find three powered dive frames," Mace said. "Use one of them." The Black Dragon laughed, an eerie sound that echoed inside Tom's helmet. "And so I get my revenge after all, since what could be crueler for someone like you than being forever in debt to your own worst enemy?"

Somewhere forward, another of the submarine's watertight bulkheads groaned under pressure and imploded with a thud. The suction nearly pulled Tom from the ladder.

"Mace!" Tom cried. "Mace, can you hear me?"

But no answer came.

The Black Dragon is dead, thought Tom. And I don't have any time to waste.

He jetted to the escape-hatch door. It was open. When disaster came to the sub, it had come too quickly for those in the after section to save themselves. Inside the compartment, just as Mace had promised, three powered dive frames hung in racks against the bulkhead.

Tom swam to one of the frames. Reversing direction with his jetpack, he maneuvered the pressure-stiffened right arm of his dive suit down into the frame and tried to flex his fingers. They moved. The power of the mechanical exoskeleton was strong enough to overcome the pressure-stiffened baroplast.

Working with his right arm in the powered suit, Tom brought his left arm into the frame. Then, using both arms, he struggled into the body of the exoskeleton. Completely mobile at last, he turned to the escape hatch's outer door and twisted the wheel to open it.

The door swung out into the sea. Tom jetted through and back to the suspended escape pod.

"Got it," Tom said over the aqualingua. "Now let me have your emergency rafts."

Working quickly, Tom attached the rafts to the outside of the pod. "Okay," he said. "This is it." One by one, Tom pulled the activation rings on the rafts. They filled slowly. "Almost, but not quite enough. The pressure's too great for them to inflate all the way. Let's get underneath and push up with our jetpacks."

"Right, Tom," Rick said. He jetted down and positioned himself beneath the pod. "Here we go."

With three half-inflated life rafts giving the pod some lift, Tom and the others were able to push it gradually upward. Tom watched the depth readout on the projection in his helmet.

"Keep pushing," he said. "It's working."

"Oh, no!" Mandy gasped. "Look down!"

Tom glanced below. The sinking submarine was now far beneath them. Its holographic sea-monster disguise flickered for a second, then shut off. A rapid series of thudding sounds came through the water as the remaining watertight bulkheads inside the submarine gave way. Silent now, the sub drifted downward and vanished into the plume of dark, mineral-laden water rising from the undersea volcanic vent.

"So much for the Black Dragon," Tom said. "In the end, failure brought him the same reward that he promised to everybody else."

But the people in the escape pod were going to make it. The pod was going up faster and faster now, and the life rafts were expanding as the pressure on them lessened. Soon the rafts were able to lift the pod on their own. Tom and the others let it go and jetted past it toward the surface.

The face of the sea was bright with sunlight as the four teens bobbed to the top of the waves. Tom looked around for the floating platform.

"There it is!" cried Mandy. "Over that way!"

They swam over to the platform and climbed up onto the deck. It didn't take long for Tom to realize that the Swift Enterprises experimental floating platform was in a bad way. It had settled until the deck was even with the surface of the ocean. Little ripples of water splashed back and forth across the deck.

Captain O'Brien and his crew and Louis Armont and his two scientists stood together on the deck near the davits. The utility boat was swung out, and Armont's bright orange data box already lay inside it.

"The platform's going down," O'Brien said. "We tried, but we couldn't save it. I'm about ready to abandon ship and take the boat to Bermuda."

"We're luckier than Xavier Mace," Tom said as he pulled off his helmet. "I'm afraid he's escaped the law again—this time permanently."

"Look!" Sandra shouted. "There comes the pod!"

Twenty yards off the starboard beam the escape pod bobbed to the surface. The top hatch opened, and a man stuck his head out.

"Ahoy the ship!" he shouted. "We surrender! Our life pod is taking on water. Will you let us come aboard?"

O'Brien looked over at Tom. "If you've brought them this far," the captain said, "you can't abandon them now."

"Right," said Tom. He grabbed a coil of line from a life-ring station and tossed one end to the floating escape pod. The man made the end fast to a ringbolt on the top of the pod. The crew of the floating platform pulled on the line and brought the pod alongside. Tom made the line fast to a cleat and stepped back.

"Okay," he said. "Come out one at a time, very slowly. Stand over there with your hands up. Otherwise, you'll have to swim back to Bermuda."

The first man climbed out and down. He was a tall, bearded man wearing a set of blue coveralls with the Black Dragon's emblem on his chest. He was followed by a short, stocky woman, also wearing blue coveralls. Then a third man stuck his head out of the hatch. It was Anton, the Black Dragon's personal bodyguard.

"Hello, Tom," Anton said in a deep, calm voice. Tom realized that this was the first time he had heard the bodyguard speak. "We owe you our lives."

"That's the way it happens sometimes," Tom replied. "Come on out and stand over there with your friends."

Anton came out, climbed down, and stood beside the other two crew members.

"Not too close," Tom cautioned him. "Was there anyone else in the escape pod?"

"Well, now that you mention it—"

"Hey, Anton, catch!" a woman's voice yelled from the pod. Tom caught a glimpse of Felicity's red hair and yellow swimsuit, and then she was tossing something blue-black and metallic through the air toward Anton.

The bodyguard caught the submachine gun and pulled back the bolt. It flew forward again with a loud *ka-chink*. He leveled the weapon at Tom and his friends.

"Stand aside from the davits," Anton said. "We're taking that boat."

15

"COME ON DOWN, FELICITY," ANTON SAID.

The redheaded woman climbed from the pod to stand beside the Black Dragon's former bodyguard.

"It wouldn't do at all for us to go on trial for piracy, murder, and so forth," Anton said. "So we're going to be taking that boat. When we arrive in Bermuda, we'll try to remember to send someone out to rescue you."

"Don't you feel any gratitude to us for saving you?" Sandra Swift demanded hotly. "If it hadn't been for us, you'd all be dead!"

"Of course I feel gratitude," Anton said. "You'll notice that you're still alive. And if you work fast, you should be able to put together a life raft out of scrap materials before the platform sinks. But this conversation has gone on long enough. We're taking the boat."

"Wait!" said Tom. "At least let me first get Louis Armont's research data out of the boat. You owe me that much, I think."

Anton and Felicity looked at each other. Felicity shrugged. "Why not?" she said. "We don't need it."

"Okay," Anton said to Tom. "You can have your precious data. Just hurry up and get it."

The waves washing back and forth across the deck of the sinking platform lapped against Tom's ankles as he crossed over to the utility boat. He climbed over the gunwale and bent down to pick up the orange plastic box that contained the data. He reached for the data box with one hand. His fingers closed around it. At the same time, with the other hand, he pulled open the utility boat's engine cover.

Anton raised the submachine gun.

"Don't shoot him, you idiot!" Felicity shouted. "If you put holes in that boat, we'll *all* drown."

Tom ignored them both. When he straightened up, he had the rotor from the engine's distributor in his hand. He held the metal part over the water.

"Shoot me, and I'll drop the rotor," Tom said. "And we'll all be stuck here together. Now put down your gun."

"Nice try," Anton said. "But not good enough. I don't have to shoot you. You can just stand there while I shoot your friends, one by one. And believe me, I will. I don't have anything to lose."

On the platform, Mandy gasped, and Louis Armont exclaimed, "You are a monster!"

"I try," said Anton. "Now, let's see. Who should I shoot first?"

The former bodyguard looked over at the hostages. "How about this one?" he said, gesturing toward Bob Weinberg with the muzzle of his submachine gun. "Or should I shoot the old man or one of the girls? Come on, boy inventor. Tell me who it's going to be."

Tom dropped the rotor into the bottom of the boat. "Okay, Anton," he said. "That's about enough."

Anton turned toward the young inventor, submachine gun at the ready. As Anton turned, Tom lifted his arm and activated the beam of his chronolaser at full power. A beam of scarlet light shot out and struck the magazine of the submachine gun.

The intense heat of the laser caused a round to cook off with a loud report, followed by two more in rapid succession. Anton dropped the now-useless weapon from stinging hands just as Rick Cantwell rushed forward and hit him with a flying tackle. The two of them toppled together onto the deck. Felicity sprang to her companion's aid, only to lose her footing when Mandy and Sandra pulled her down. The two remaining coverall-clad submariners raised their hands.

"Don't hurt us," the man said. "All we did was run the sub. We never had anything to do with the rest."

"That'll be for a court to decide," Captain O'Brien said. "Turn around, both of you. Get down on your knees with your hands on top of your heads. Booth, get some line and tie them up. Tom, thanks for some good thinking back there."

The four surviving members of the Black Dragon's staff were soon tied up. Lloyd Jones, the platform engineer, fished the distributor rotor out of the bottom of the utility boat and put it back into place. By then, the water was up to knee level on the deck of the floating platform.

"We're going down pretty fast," Captain O'Brien said. "Let's hit the boat."

Tom and Rick brought the tied prisoners into the utility boat and put them near the bow. Then the rest of the party got aboard. Katie Booth cast them off and took the boat away from the floating platform. They stood by at a safe distance, watching the platform slip below the waves. At last even the superstructure dropped out of sight.

"Okay, time to go," O'Brien said. "Next stop, Bermuda."

"What's that?" Sandra asked, pointing west and shading her eyes with her other hand.

"Looks like a couple of inbound helicopters," Tom replied.

Indeed they were: a gray Navy CH-46 Sea Knight and a green Marine Corps AH1–Huey Cobra gunship. The CH-46 hovered overhead, and a voice blared over its outside speakers: "We got word from a patrol aircraft that you were in trouble. Do you require assistance?"

"That's a negative," Tom yelled back. "The situation here is entirely under control."

That same evening found Tom and his friends—and Lieutenant Commanders Pena and Otano from the naval air station—gathered around a large table in the Courtyard, the finest restaurant in Hamilton, Bermuda. Large bronze chandeliers hung from the cypress ceiling beams, shining on a table laden with plates of fish chowder, Bermuda rockfish, and cassava pie.

"I've heard from my father," Tom was saying to Lieutenant Commander Pena. "All of those ships that were sunk in the area over the past year were owned, one way or another, by the Black Dragon, through a variety of holding companies and false fronts. That's how he arranged to have them come by at the right place and the right time, with the right cargoes in their holds."

"But why?" Rick asked. "He was rich enough. Why not just buy the stuff and ship it out?"

"When the ships vanished in the Bermuda Triangle," Tom said, "the different companies would file insurance claims. That way Mace would get to keep the cargoes and would get reimbursed for them, too. In effect, he was getting his supplies for free and smuggling in his divers and other specialists that way, too, as part of the ships' crews."

Captain O'Brien nodded. "And anybody on board who wasn't already working for Xavier Mace was offered the Black Dragon's version of the traditional pirates' choice: sign up or swim home."

"When Mace found the tectonic plate under Bermuda," Tom continued, "and started his project to raise up a new country out of the ocean, he must have decided to use the Triangle legend to cover his tracks."

"Dad always said that Xavier Mace couldn't resist any plan that could make him money," said Sandra. "And if it was illegal, so much the better."

"Well, that base of his is finished for good," Lieutenant Commander Otano said from the other side of the table. "The navy's going to be holding live-fire depth-charge drills tomorrow, and by one of life's eerie coincidences, the place we've decided to use is the location of the Black Dragon's undersea headquarters."

"But what will stop someone else from doing the same thing as Mace someday?" Sandra asked. "There are other criminals in the world. Maybe another one will want to make an island that no country has ever claimed."

"Not too likely," Louis Armont said. "The last bits of data that I collected, just before the Black Dragon sabotaged the platform— tell her, Bob."

"It's like this," Bob Weinberg said. "The survey we just completed has far more detail than any survey done before in this area. Better even than the information Mace was using to make his plans, as it turns out. That fault line he was going to use for making his new island turned out to be a combination of errors on the part of the original mapmaker and wishful thinking on Mace's part. All that his explosion would have done is hit Bermuda with a tidal wave, possibly killing upward of fifty thousand people."

"That's bad enough, thank you," said Mandy. "But you're right. It wouldn't have given him the island kingdom he dreamed of."

"Then he would have just come up with another plan, somewhere else, some other time," Tom said. "Mace was, if anything, inventive." He shook his head thoughtfully. "But you know, I still don't know what he looked like. With those holographic disguises of his, every time I saw him he looked different."

"So it goes," said Rick Cantwell. "But it certainly looks like we're stuck on shore for the rest of our vacation. Maybe *now* I'll have a chance to see some really good-looking girls."

The other members of the dinner party didn't move fast enough as Sandra, right in the middle of Bermuda's fanciest restaurant, dumped a tall glass of iced tea on Rick's head.

Tom's next adventure:

Tom Swift has developed an ultrapowerful tele-
scopic device that promises to yield dramatic
new insight into the deepest mysteries of the
universe. But his first discovery is no more than
two hundred miles up, and it's a shocker. A tiny
cube of polished granite is orbiting the earth,
and on its side Tom spots a message—in a language no one has ever encountered before!

Tom's infrared photo of the object convinces a
friend at NASA to use an all-new Swift-
enhanced space shuttle to retrieve the mystery
stone, but the flight ultimately leads Tom to the
surface of the moon. A force of unknown origin,
controlled by a hidden intelligence, has lured
the mission into an odyssey of danger . . . in
Tom Swift #7, *Moonstalker.*